diary of a 6th grade ninja 5

terror at the talent show

BY MARCUS EMERSON
AND NOAH CHILD

ILLUSTRATED BY DAVID LEE

EMERSON PUBLISHING HOUSE

This one's for Elijah...

This book is a work of fiction. Names, characters, places, and incidents are the product of the author's imagination or are used fictitiously. Any resemblance to actual events, locales, or persons, living or dead, is coincidental.

My name is Chase Cooper, and I'm a sixth grader at Buchanan School. That's a photo of me up there studying for a big test – wait, no. That's a penguin. My photo is on the next page.

If you're reading this then you probably know who I am, but for those of you who don't, allow me to give you the super jacked turbo version.

I'm an eleven-year-old sixth grader at Buchanan School. My favorite foods are cheese pizza, grilled cheese sandwiches, and nachos with extra cheese.

I love watching awful horror movies from the '90s, corny action movies from the '80s, and the absolute worst science fiction movies from the '70s. And I mean the worst of the worst – spaceships on strings and alien costumes where you can see the zipper.

What else do I do? Well, I spend most of my free time playing video games and reading comics, y'know, typical sixth grader things. Sometimes I'll throw a book or two into the mix, just to make things interesting. It's a personal goal of mine to read at least fifty books this year. Why? Why not? Being dumb is dumb, and smart is the new cool.

ME PLAYING ~~VIDEO~~ ~~GAMES~~ STUDYING

CHASE COOPER

Additional things I enjoy include riding my bike through trails in the woods, swimming, climbing things, eating cookies with orange soda, tormenting my little sister, and leading a ninja clan to defend my school against evil...

Oh, right. There's also *that*.

I'm a ninja.

I was the new kid at the beginning of year and was recruited by a secret ninja clan that met during my gym class. My first baby ninja steps were pretty wobbly, but I think I handled myself alright. After saving the day by uncovering a shady plot to frame my cousin for theft, the ninja clan thought it'd be a good idea if I were their new leader.

(NINJA DOVES ADDED FOR EFFECT)

(Because they're super cool)

I've been struggling to be a good leader, and I'm the first to admit that I've failed more than a few times. But life lessons were dished out, and I learned a lot, which hopefully makes me a more experienced leader now. I don't know. I'm still just doing my best to make it to the end of the year without a broken face.

It's only been two weeks since Jovial Noise tried messing up the science fair. Her real name is Olivia Jones, but she calls herself Jovial Noise – I think it has something to do with her desire to be a villain or something. She left notes in my locker every day, challenging me to play along in her sinister game. In the end, good prevailed over evil, and the science fair had been saved.

Normally, Buchanan School liked to take a month long break between the times it was trying to shake up my world, but I had a feeling that was starting to change. I couldn't put my finger on it, but something was already off the second I shut the door to my dad's car.

My dad dropped me off by the side doors of the school a little earlier than normal. I needed to get to my locker and pay a visit to Zoe before seeing her in homeroom because I had to... well, to be honest, I wanted to *apologize* to her.

Let me explain – the Buchanan Talent show was coming up on Friday, and she was put in charge of it. Yep – the *entire* thing. Buchanan wasn't even going to *have* a talent show until Zoe begged Principal Davis to have one. He said the only way he would even *consider* it would be if one of the students took charge and planned it on their own. Obviously Zoe jumped at the chance to do it. I'm pretty sure she knew how much work she'd have to put in, but she's the kind of kid that *likes* that sort of work. The coolest part about the whole thing is that Principal Davis moved some funding around and has offered a thousand dollar grand prize for the winner.

On Saturday, she called my cellphone and asked me to help. This was our conversation...

"Hey, Chase," Zoe said over the phone. "Wanna come help set up the cafeteria for the talent show? We're meeting at noon. Faaaaaaaith will be there."

"Yeah?" I asked, holding my phone between my head and shoulder so both my hands would be free to keep playing my video game.

"Yep!" Zoe said joyfully. "Gavin'll be there too. You can call Brayden if you want."

I sighed. It sounded alright until she said Gavin *was going to be there. That's just how I wanted to spend my Saturday - sitting around at school watching my cousin and her boyfriend hold hands and giggle at each other. Sick. "Sorry, Zoe," I said. "I totally would, but did you say noon? Yeeeeeah, that's actually right in the middle of my nap, so I'm gonna have to say no. Maybe next time."*

Zoe paused over the phone. "But the stage needs some work and Gavin said it'd be easy to set up with a few extra kids there. Can't you skip your nap to help?"

"Nope," I said flatly.

"But you're like eleven-years-old," *Zoe said. "Didn't you stop taking naps in kindergarten?"*

4

"You know I gotta take advantage of Saturday naps while I can!"

"...serious?" Zoe asked, shocked.

"Mm hmm," I hummed, listening to her end of the line click as she hung up on me.

So yeah, that happened over the weekend and I've felt guilty ever since.

After my nap, I texted her, but she never replied. I thought I'd get a chance to say sorry at Sunday brunch, but she skipped to keep setting up for the talent show, and that's the reason I was early to school on a Monday morning.

I opened the side doors to the school and stepped into the hallway. It was only 7:30 in the morning so homeroom wasn't for another fifteen minutes. I had my dad drop me off early and on the side of the school so I could get to my locker before going to the cafeteria to talk to Zoe, but I'm not a morning person so I was really dragging.

As soon as the doors shut, I felt a chill dance down my spine. It was as if Buchanan School was teasing at the fact that I was going to face some serious trials this week. I *knew* the actual fifteenth president of the United States *wasn't* a ghost out to get me, but I still balled my fist and hissed, *"James Buchanan!"*

Shaking the chills off my back, I shuffled my feet across the carpet, feeling the weight of my drowsiness settling in on my eyelids. Man, no matter how hard I tried, I just couldn't get my blood pumping! I was *tired*, but not just a little tired. Like, *tired* tired.

Like, the kind of tired where my head bobs up and down until my whole body jerks awake and then I realize everyone in math is staring at me, wondering how an eleven-year-old kid could possibly produce the amount of drool that was pooled on my desk and... nevermind. Let's just say I felt like a zombie.

As I approached my locker, I clenched my jaw and gulped. Every time I opened it, my heart still raced at the thought of finding another sticky note with a chess piece. Olive's notes had stopped after she got busted, but I still couldn't help but worry.

Spinning the combination into the lock, I pulled up on the handle and flipped the door wide open, flinching as if a clown on a spring was going to jump at me.

But it was all clear. I smiled, finally able to breathe again as I stared at the trash heap that was collecting in my locker. There wasn't anything out of the ordinary about any of it, except for the few spots of mold that looked like they had started growing hair and teeth.

I stuffed my textbooks into my book bag and zipped it up. As I slung the strap over my shoulder, I heard some commotion down the hall. It was hard to make out what they were saying from where I was standing, but one sentence came through crystal clear.

"That penguin got out of its cage!"

Did that boy just say *penguin?* Shutting my locker, I leaned back, making that *"huh?"* face I make when I'm totally confused about something. You know the one – you've probably made the same face when you've smelled something nasty, but couldn't figure out *what* it was. Yeah, *that* face.

I followed the other students as they ran to the tinted glass walls of the cafeteria. The sound of excited shouts bounced down the hallway, growing louder as I walked closer.

"Look at them chase after the penguin!"

There it was again! The mention of the penguin along with a chorus of laughter from the crowd of students in the lobby. I had no idea what was happening, but felt the sudden rush of excitement pour over me, completely shocking my body out of its drowsy state.

Stepping into the lobby of the school, I made my way through the swarm of kids. A chill ran down my spine like it had when I first entered the building, but I wasn't sure whether to be worried or not because half the students around me were laughing, while the other half looked frightened.

As I approached the cafeteria doors, I saw a line of boys and girls with their faces pressed against the glass, trying their best to see what was going on.

I'm not sure why, but I glanced at the clock. I *knew* it was only 7:35 in the morning, and I *knew* that Zoe would be in the cafeteria setting up for the talent show, but part of me hoped that maybe it was later in the morning and my cousin would be out of the cafeteria already, safe from the ruckus. No such luck though.

Pressing my face against the door of the lunchroom, I squinted to see through the thin pane of glass while students beside me spoke out loud.

"*What happened to the penguin? Does anybody see the penguin anymore?*"

"*I think it went under the stage!*"

"*Who's Zoe chasing after? Is that dude gliding on the floor? It looks like he's flying!*"

And then I heard a loud crash come from inside the cafeteria. Everyone in the lobby gasped.

"*Watch out! He's coming at the door!*" a girl right next to me shouted.

I tried to dive out of the way, but it was too late. The doors to the cafeteria burst open, knocking me clear across the lobby. Rolling across the floor, I felt the carpet burn my elbows until I finally stopped against the wall.

"Outta my way!" shouted a voice.

I glanced up just in time to see a boy skid along the carpet on one of those scooters that folded up. He was wearing a white hockey mask so no one could see his face.

"Chase!" shouted a familiar voice by the cafeteria doors.

Shaking my head, I jumped to my feet, baffled by what was happening. Gavin was running out of the cafeteria with two folded up scooters, one in each hand. Other students down the hallway were screaming at the boy in the hockey mask. Because of the crowded corridor, he hadn't gotten far yet.

Gavin chucked one of the folded scooters at my feet, and then flipped open the locked hinge on his scooter, shooting the wheels out from under it. "There's no time to explain!" he shouted. "Come on!"

I kicked at the end of my scooter, popping the whole thing off the ground. I grabbed the handle bar with my right hand, and hopped into air, using my foot to open the locked hinge. The scooter twisted open like a set of nun chucks and snapped into shape as I nailed the landing on the carpet of the lobby. I stood there for a moment, surprised that the scooter didn't slip out from under me.

I laughed so hard that I snorted, amazed by my crazy good luck. "Ha!" I barked as I looked around. "*Did anyone else just see that?*"

All the students in the lobby were too busy staring down the hall, watching Gavin chase after the boy in the hockey mask. Not a single other kid was looking in my direction.

"*Seriously?*" I said, grinding my teeth. "One of the *sickest* stunts I've ever done in front of dozens of people, and *nobody* saw it! *Just* my luck!"

Kicking the carpet, I shot the scooter forward, weaving through the crowd of students. Gavin was about twenty feet ahead of me, and I could see the boy in the hockey mask just a little bit in front of him.

As kids dove out of the way, I kept kicking at the floor, making my sweet ride roll faster. Finally, I caught up to Gavin's side.

"What's the deal?" I yelled, gripping my handlebars tighter.

Gavin kept his eyes on the kid in the hockey mask. "That doofus set a penguin loose in the cafeteria!"

"What's a penguin even doing in school?" I asked, leaning to my left and barely dodging a girl. She spun in a circle, dropping a few of her textbooks as I passed her.

"Watch it!" she shouted, annoyed.

"Sorry!" I hollered.

Gavin stomped his foot harder on the carpet, getting his

scooter up to epic speeds. "The penguin was part of some kid's talent show performance or something! Zoe had all the acts show up early today so we could test out the stage and make sure it was solid!"

"Someone's got a penguin in the talent show?" I asked.

"I guess it dances with them or something," Gavin replied. "Whoever this kid is we're chasin' after is the one that popped open the cage and set it free!"

Staring ahead of us, I saw that the kid had turned down another hallway. "Why would he do that?"

As Gavin neared the corner, he jumped off his scooter and started sprinting down the new hallway. Once a couple of students were out of the way, he rolled the scooter on the floor and hopped back on at full speed. I'm not gonna lie – it was awesome.

I followed his lead and tried to the do the exact same thing, except my moves weren't as gazelle-like. Instead, I took the corner too fast and bounced off the lockers like a ragdoll. I regained my balance and jumped back on my scooter, hoping no one saw my goof. It took a few good kicks to catch up with Gavin again.

The new hallway wasn't carpeted so our rubber wheels picked up even more speed. I'd never had a bike or skateboard in school so the whole thing was exciting. Our scooters almost glided like they didn't have wheels at all.

The kid in the hockey was still ahead of us. Every so often, he'd glance over his shoulder to make sure we were still far behind. Whoever it was must've had some pretty strong legs because they seemed to have no problem maintaining the gap between us.

Gavin continued. "Right after everyone freaked out that the penguin was loose, one of the corners on the stage collapsed. Luckily the thing's only a foot off the floor or it could've done some minor damage."

"Ya think the kid had something to do with the stage?" I asked, kicking the polished floor beneath my shoe.

"Definitely!" Gavin said confidently. "Once that penguin got loose, the stage collapsed, and as soon as the stage collapsed, that kid grabbed a scooter and bolted out the door."

"Where'd these scooters come from—" I started to ask, but was interrupted.

A hand grabbed at the collar of my shirt, yanking me off my scooter, not hard enough to hurt, but just enough to stop me in my tracks. I looked up and saw Principal Davis looking rather disappointed at me. Mrs. Olsen, the science teacher, was standing in front of Gavin, blocking his path with her hands on her hips.

"These scooters are from the drama department," Principal Davis grunted.

I looked down the hall, but saw no sign of the kid in the hockey mask. "But the kid in the mask is getting away!" I shouted. "We almost had him!"

Principal Davis furrowed his brow. "Catching him *isn't* your job. You *do* understand that, right?"

I sighed, staring at the floor and nodding.

Gavin fell silent and stared at the same spot on floor.

The principal folded his arms and chewed his lip. "Look, I get it. I know you just want to help your cousin, but this kind of thing is better left to the adults, alright? You could've hurt someone tearing through the hallways on these things, you know that?"

"Yes, sir," Gavin and I both whispered at the same time.

Mrs. Olsen huffed as she pressed her lips together, but didn't say anything.

"Why don't the two of you head back to the cafeteria," Principal Davis said. "Mrs. Olsen and I will handle things from here, alright?"

"Yes, sir," Gavin and I whispered again, shuffling our feet along the floor.

"But school's about to start," Gavin said.

Principal Davis patted at the air. "I'll have a hall monitor let your homeroom teachers know you two are helping with the talent show. You guys will be excused from class this morning."

"One of *Wyatt's* hall monitors?" Gavin sneered.

The principal nodded.

I swallowed hard, feeling a lump travel all the way down my throat, but I didn't say anything. It wasn't the time or place to mention my feud with Wyatt, the leader of the red ninja clan.

After I became the leader of Wyatt's old ninja clan, he was quick to create another one of his own. My ninjas are honorable and strive to do the right thing, but his ninjas are another story. They exist to wreak havoc and create chaos wherever they are. They have chased me on more than one occasion since they emerged from the depths of Buchanan School.

Gavin and I were instructed to leave our scooters behind. Principal Davis said he'd personally return them to the drama club later on. I'm pretty sure it was because he didn't trust that Gavin and I wouldn't ride them in the halls again, and I don't blame him for thinking that because we totally would've.

"I can't believe that kid got away," Gavin mumbled. "That's the sorta thing that really grinds my gears, y'know?"

"Yeah," I sighed. "And I'm not sure that Principal Davis is gonna be able to catch him."

"What he'll likely do is assign the case to the hall monitors," Gavin said. "Which normally woulda been a good idea, but ever since Wyatt took over, I'm not sure how much help *they* are anymore."

"They're all red ninjas," I said. "Remember the red wrist bands?"

Once Wyatt took Gavin's place as the hall monitor captain,

11

things have been going downhill. Wyatt had replaced *every* normal hall monitor with a member of the red ninja clan. Yep, red ninjas walk the halls of Buchanan right out in the open and in their normal street clothes. They can tell each other apart from the red wrist bands they all wear. I haven't been able to prove anything yet, but I just *know* Wyatt is planning something big. He's *gotta* be!

And Sebastian, the school president, *has* to be in on it. He's the one who fired Gavin and promoted Wyatt, but nobody has any idea why! Sebastian was known for being a flaky kid and so was Wyatt, so the two of them working together equals some sort of mega ultra super villain duo, bent on school domination!

Gavin nodded at me. "Yeah, I remember those wrist bands. You don't suppose Wyatt was the kid we were just chasin' after, do ya?"

"On the scooter?" I asked, suddenly floored that I hadn't even considered that yet. "It makes perfect sense, doesn't it? He stole my book bag a couple of months ago and took off down the hallway just like the kid in the hockey mask!"

"That kid had some moves too."

"Wyatt? Or Hockey Mask?" I asked, smiling smugly at the nickname I thought up for the mystery kid.

"*Both*," Gavin replied, turning down the hallway that led back to the cafeteria.

"Great!" I said. "Then all we have to do is prove Wyatt was in the cafeteria *before* the penguin was set free, and then question where he was *after* all that jazz. We should be able to connect enough dots for Principal Davis to bust him once and for all!"

Gavin nodded.

At that moment, the bell chimed overhead. The school day had officially started. Gavin and I started jogging to the cafeteria. Principal Davis said it was cool for us to skip homeroom, and anytime I'm told to skip a class by the principal, you better believe I'm gonna do it.

12

Monday. 7:46 AM. The cafeteria.

Gavin made it to the cafeteria doors first and held them open for me. As I stepped through, I saw the mini stage Zoe was trying to get built. It wasn't a full stage like I thought it was, but merely an extension of the stage that was already there. It was a platform that stuck out about eight feet, but one of the corners was leaning on the ground. That must've been where it was sabotaged.

On the polished floor were skid lines from the scooter that Hockey Mask had used to escape. I followed the lines all the way back to a long bench against the far wall.

Lining the bench were students who I assumed had acts in the talent show. It must've been where they waited for their turn. The bench and all the kids sat under a huge metal scaffolding, the kind that painters stand on to reach high places. The wooden board and paint cans on top were tipped to the side. Luckily none of the paint had spilled. That would have been disastrous.

Against the wall, I saw my cousin sitting on the floor and hugging her knees. Her face was red from crying. Her hands were balled into little fists, pinching the ends of her sleeves that she used to wipe her tears away. Faith and some other girls were by her side, comforting her.

Across the room, I saw the metal cage that must've had the penguin in it. The student that owned the penguin was sitting in her chair and staring at the cage in disbelief. I recognized her immediately. Her name was Sophia, and she was one of Buchanan's star cello players. She dressed super trendy, like she

13

was straight out of a teenybopper magazine for young hipsters.

"How's a kid own a penguin anyway?" I asked Gavin.

Gavin shrugged his shoulders. "I dunno, but probably the same way some folks own monkeys."

I shook my head, smirking. "Man, *that'd* be cool, huh? A *monkey*. I'd totally train it in the art of ninjutsu. Can you imagine that? A tiny monkey ninja sidekick that drops in at the first sign of trouble?"

Gavin stared at me for a second. "That's the dumbest thing I've ever heard."

I tightened my lips, slightly embarrassed.

Zoe's voice cut through the air like a katana. "This is *your* fault!"

I spun around, surprised and scared by her sudden outburst. "Mine?"

My cousin jumped up from the floor and stormed toward me with her finger pointing directly at me face. "If you had been here over the weekend to help, then *none* of this would've happened!"

"What?" I cried defensively.

Zoe whipped her hand out and pointed at the stage. "The only reason why that thing isn't finished yet was because we didn't have enough people to help! If you were here, it would've been finished, and none of this would've happened!"

Gavin set his foot up on a chair and leaned against his knee like a cowboy. "She's got a point. The only reason why the corner buckled the way it did was 'cause it wasn't latched into place – none of the corners are. I needed an extra pair of hands to do it so it had to wait until this week."

I stared at the stage, shocked. I didn't know what to say. "But I'm here now. Can't we fix it?"

Gavin leaned over and studied the collapsed portion of the stage. "Nope," he said flatly. "We're gonna have to order a new part for it. This one's busted up now."

Zoe turned back toward me and jabbed at my chest with her finger. "Which means the stage is going to remain incomplete for the entire week! And you know what *that* means…"

I stared into my cousin's fiery eyes. She's a bit of a perfectionist to the point of actually being insane. She's the kind of kid who finishes her homework *weeks* before it's due – the kind of kid that makes a hundred lists for any sort of activity she's involved in – the kind of kid that prints out a schedule for the family when we go on trips – the kind of kid that finishes every single task she's given, on time, and flawlessly – the kind of kid that… you get the point.

An unfinished piece of her talent show puzzle was going to have her pulling her hair out all week. It was very possible that she was going to look like an old bald man by Friday.

"I'm sorry," I whispered, and then I remembered the conversation Gavin and I had in the hall about Wyatt. "But Gavin and I both think we know who freed the penguin and broke the stage!"

"Oh really?" said a high-pitched voice from behind me. "And just who do you think the guilty student is?"

I slowly turned around, but already knew who it was. It was Wyatt, leader of the red ninja clan and captain of the hall monitors.

"Wyatt," I said, clenching my jaw.

"S'up, yo?" Wyatt replied with a mouthful of bubblegum, nodding his chin at me.

"I don't know how you got back here so fast," I said, "but I *know* it was you that broke the stage."

Wyatt pushed the huge wad of pink gum into the side of his cheek making it look like he had a golf ball in his mouth. "I've been in here the entire time!" he laughed loudly.

Zoe folded her arms. "He's telling the truth," she said. "He's been at one of the tables in the corner with his cousin, Carlyle. They're one of the acts in the show."

"Har!" Carlyle shouted as he ran forward.

Carlyle was a problem during my second month at Buchanan. He acts, dresses, and talks like a pirate in every annoying way possible. His plan was to change the school mascot to The Buccaneers, which would mean our school would've officially been a pirate themed school. Thankfully, I was able to stop it from happening.

"Seems like your facts be a little off, eh matey?" Carlyle sneered, squinting an eye at me.

I grit my teeth, super annoyed by the way he spoke. "Seems *like*," I said.

WYATT
(ninja)

CARLYLE
(Pirate)

Gavin's face twisted. I could tell he was upset that our

assumption of Wyatt being guilty was wrong.

Carlyle stepped forward and put his hand on his cousin's shoulder. "I'll do ya one better, mate. My cousin and I even tried to *catch* that sea-snarfin' penguin when it escaped!"

"It's true," Faith said, standing by Zoe's side. "Wyatt was actually the first one to jump after it."

"Really," Gavin said somberly. "That don't sound like somethin' you'd do."

Wyatt tilted his head slightly and smiled. "Don't know if you heard yet, but I'm the hall monitor captain now. I got a reputation to uphold."

I watched the muscles in Gavin's jaw twitch, but he remained silent. Wyatt had just dealt a low blow to my friend.

Zoe finally spoke, cutting through the awkward silence. "Whatever, alright? What happened has already happened. The only thing we can do now is clean up and try to fix things before this Friday. The good news is that we have a week to sort it out."

Wyatt and Carlyle laughed and stepped out of the cafeteria. With Wyatt as the hall monitor captain now, it probably wasn't too difficult for him to skip class without a pass.

Zoe, Faith, and their friends went back to the stage. They were in the middle of painting oversized banners that were resting on the floor. Zoe had chosen a bright orange color to use for all the talent show posters. She had always been good at artsy stuff like that.

The student with the penguin was talking to Principal Davis, probably giving him a detailed report of when the animal was last seen and which direction it ran away in. Just what Buchanan School needed – a loose penguin poopin' all over the place.

"So we were wrong," Gavin said as he approached me.

I hated to admit it, but it was the truth. "Yup," I said.

"Principal Davis said he'd handle it, and I'm inclined to believe everything he says being that he's the *principal* and all," Gavin said.

Staring at the floor, it took all my concentration to understand what Gavin was saying since he talked like a cowboy. He *was* from Texas after all, but I'm pretty sure they stopped talking like that back in the 1800's. "Right," I replied.

"But that don't mean we can't *help* the case," Gavin said.

"Wyatt might not have done it, but *somebody* did."

"Obviously," I said. "We weren't chasing after a ghost or... *were we?*" I snapped my head to the side, half expecting to see the ghost of James Buchanan laughing at me from the corner of the cafeteria.

"I say we team up and try to figure this thing out on our own," Gavin said, pointing his finger back and forth between us. "But Zoe ain't gonna be happy 'bout that."

"Why would she care what you did?" I asked, but already knew the answer before I finished speaking.

Gavin paused. "Because we're goin' out now."

Guh. I wasn't sure why I felt uncomfortable, but there wasn't anything I could do about it. Maybe it was because she was my cousin, and I felt like I had to protect her. Gavin was a good guy though – it wasn't like she was going out with *Wyatt*.

I faked a smile and nodded. Then I changed the subject back to what we were talking about. "I'm not sure what we can do to help find Hockey Mask."

"We can ask around," Gavin said, taking a breath. "At this point, the crime has been committed. We'll look for clues and talk to some kids who might've seen something."

"Okay," I said. "Where do we start?"

Gavin looked at the empty penguin cage across the room. "Seein' as it's Sophia's penguin, I think we should ask her first."

I turned my head, looking for the girl in trendy clothing, but she wasn't in the room anymore. "Great," I said. "Where'd she go?"

Gavin raised his eyebrows. "She's probably in the principal's office now. I'm sure her parents are already on their way here. We'll have to catch her at lunch."

"That'll be good," I said. "I'm sure she'll have her penguin back by then. Meet me in the lobby before lunch?"

"Yep." Gavin nodded as he walked away. "See ya then."

I tightened my grip around my book bag straps and walked out of the cafeteria. Homeroom was just about over so first period was coming up. I had a few minutes of alone time before the bell went off so I spent it on a bench in the lobby, staring at the dark red carpet where I was knocked over.

I felt awful about letting Zoe down. If I had come and

helped over the weekend, none of this might've even happened. *That* was the real reason I wanted to find Hockey Mask, not because I wanted to bust him, but because I felt like I owed it to my cousin. She worked harder than anyone I knew, and she totally didn't deserve this. She's nice to everyone, even if they were jerks to her.

The past few incidents at Buchanan always revolved around me so it was easy for me to brush the dirt off my chin and get back on my feet, but this time was different. This time it involved my family.

Monday. 10:46 AM. Gym class.

For the first time in my life, I was looking forward to gym. The morning was still a whirlwind of events bouncing around my noggin so I thought getting some fresh air while walking the track might help clear my mind. Good thing Mr. Cooper, the gym coach, pretty much allowed us to do whatever we wanted.

I was really hoping to see Zoe in first period art since we had that class together, but she was allowed to skip and keep working on talent show stuff. Maybe it was a good thing I didn't see her though – I *wanted* to say something about how Gavin and I were going to scope things out on our own, but after thinking about it for an hour, it might actually just make her more angry.

I leaned against the wall, watching as students walked out of the locker rooms. Could the kid in the hockey mask be one of them? Was he watching me right now, laughing on the inside at the fact that he got away?

"Hey, man," a boy's voice said.

I shook my head, coming back to reality. In the short amount of time I zoned out, my best friend, Brayden, had taken the spot next to me.

An interesting bit of information about Brayden – he's a self-proclaimed werewolf hunter, but has never found a werewolf before. Trust me when I say it's not that he hasn't tried. His basement is filled with maps of upper Wisconsin that have red thumbtacks pressed into the spots where someone reported seeing a werewolf. Newspaper clippings and photocopies of books are taped to the walls like wallpaper. If anyone was going to find one of those monsters someday, it was going to be him.

"Braaaaaaayden," I sang, jokingly. "Whuddup?"

Brayden's face squirmed. I could tell he was uncomfortable.

"Something wrong?" I asked.

"I dunno, dude," Brayden said. "Somethin' about a penguin running loose in the school has me a little freaked out."

I laughed. "*That's* what's making you weird?" My back was starting to hurt where it was leaning against the wall so I put both of my hands behind me, using them for a cushion. "I bet they find that thing by the end of the day."

"But what if they *don't?*" Brayden whispered with fear in his eyes.

I paused, a little taken back by the fact that my best friend Brayden, the werewolf hunter, was afraid of a tiny little penguin. "Are you messing with me?"

Brayden gulped, and then snapped his attention to a spot across the room, the way a dog does when it sees a rabbit. After a moment, he said, "Penguins freak me out. That's all. It's not weird."

"It *is* weird," I said, smirking. "Penguins are just birds that can't fly."

"I know, man," Brayden said. "But *that's* the thing that freaks me out – what bird *can't* fly?"

"Fat birds?" I joked.

"They're up to something..." Brayden said, his voice trailing off. "Those things are smarter than you think."

"Yes," I said, agreeing with my best friend. "Every penguin on Earth is conspiring to take over the world by fooling all of humanity that they can't fly. One day we'll look to the skies and see that it's been painted black by the bodies of penguins that have taken flight, declaring war on humanity. And our children will weep as we collectively cry '*Help! Please, save us!*' But the Earth will turn its cheek from us, shut its eyes, and whisper, '*no.*'"

One of the girls standing nearby stared at me with her jaw dropped. "That's so dark," she whispered.

"*Ninja* dark," I said.

"Ninja *dork*," Brayden said, leaning against the wall. It was obvious he was joking with me because he was also in my ninja clan.

The bell rang at last as the rest of my classmates stood in a line against the wall. We had our spots memorized from having stood in them for the past few months. Mr. Cooper, the gym teacher, was normally slow to come out of his office and take attendance. Sometimes it even got to the point where some of the students would just skip roll call and start playing basketball.

"Hey, Chase!" a boy to my left said.

I spun around to see who needed me. It was Jake, followed by his wolf pack. Jake was one of the more popular kids on the football team. You know the type – tall, good looking, perfectly tousled hair, the star quarterback with the cheerleader girlfriend. A few of his jock friends trailed behind him as if they were wolves following their leader, which is why a lot of the school referred to them as the "wolf pack."

"Hi, Jake," I said.

Brayden wrinkled his nose, but didn't say anything

"Or should I call you 'moose-man?'" Jake asked. His wolf pack laughed, throwing light punches at each other's shoulders. "Way to mess up the school's mascot."

Let me explain real quick – remember when I said I was able to stop the school from becoming the Buchanan Buccaneers? Well, because of that, I was allowed to choose the new school mascot. But being who I am, I gave it *way* too much thought, and made the poor choice of casting a *moose* to represent the identity of Buchanan School. Of course now I see it was a huge mistake, but at the time, I was over the moon with excitement!

"What's done is done," I said in a monotone voice, trying to mask my fear. "If I could go back and do it again, I'd pick something cooler."

"But ya can't go back," Jake said. "Can you?"

I shook my head. "No," I whispered.

Brayden continued to say nothing.

"Leave it up to a *nerd* to choose something so lame," Jake said. "No, I'm sorry, you're not even a *nerd*. You're *less than* a nerd! You're a *nerdling*, hoping to pull yourself out of the nerd-nest to spread your nerd-wings and fly to nerd-topia!"

My jaw dropped, in awe of how poetic Jake was with his words. I tried to think of a witty comeback, but I was always bad at it when put on the spot, plus I didn't really like being a jerk. So I said, "Yeah? Well your mom called and uh… she said you'd make a very fine gentleman one day."

Jake gawked at me like a confused horse.

Brayden leaned closer and whispered. "Dude, that wasn't really a burn. That was more of a *healing* statement."

"*I know!*" I whispered back.

"Like, if this were a video game, you'd have just handed Jake a health pack," Brayden added.

I rolled my eyes.

Coach Cooper stepped out of the locker room with his clipboard in hand. As he scanned the gymnasium full of students, I could see him scratch their names off his list the same way he did every day.

Jake and his wolf pack backed away from me once Coach Cooper started walking toward the center of the gym.

23

"Listen up, everyone," the coach yelled loudly. "We'll be doing things a little different this week."

I bounced forward from the wall and stood straight up. What was he talking about? Different? Change? No! Change is bad! Change is my third greatest fear, right under spiders, and clowns on their lunch break! What? Have *you* ever seen a clown casually eating a chicken wing? Yeah, I didn't think so.

"Principal Davis has insisted on actually requiring a *little* bit of sports activity in the way I teach," the coach said. "So for the week, you'll *all* be playing football."

My stomach sunk. The only thing I understood from football was that pressing B on the controller made my quarterback chuck the ball at the nearest available teammate!

The coach pointed his finger at Jake and then made a motion telling Jake to stand next to him. Pointing his finger at Brayden, he made the same motion. Brayden glanced at me as he walked out to the center of the gym.

"These two are your team captains," Coach Cooper said. "After your teams are chosen, meet on the field outside."

Normally, I would've felt a little worried about getting picked last, but with Brayden as one of the captains, I wasn't concerned. I breathed a sigh of relief and rested against the wall again.

"Tim," Jake said, pointing to one of the boys in his wolf pack.

Here we go. Brayden's going to point at me and—

"Claire," Brayden said quickly.

I had already taken a step so I had to stop myself. It was obvious enough to be embarrassing. A few students around me chuckled to themselves. Even Claire giggled as she took her place behind Brayden.

I tightened a smile. It was cool. Brayden knew what he was doing. I'd get picked second or third, right? That's *gotta* be what he had planned... right? Hello?

Jake pointed at another boy from his wolf pack. "Zach."

Instantly, Brayden spoke. "Doug."

Just so you know, Doug is *not* my name. What was Brayden doing? After every kid he chose that *wasn't* me, he stared at the ground. And it went on like this for the next *twenty* kids that were

24

chosen! Suddenly, I was one of the three remaining students left against the wall. What gives?

Jake scratched at his chin, and then pointed at the short kid next to me. "Him," Jake said. How awful. Jake didn't even know the kid's name. I didn't either, but we'll just ignore that.

Brayden made eye contact with me, but immediately looked away. "Charlie," he said softly.

"*Really?*" I shouted, my voice echoing across the gym. I cupped my hand over my mouth, feeling stupid. Shaking my head, I started walking toward Jake's team.

"What do you think you're doing?" Jake asked. "Teams are even. Get lost."

I froze in place. I could feel everyone in the gym stare at me. You know what's bad? Getting chosen *last* for a team. You what's worse? *Not getting chosen at all.*

The other students filed out the gym doors, making their way to the football field outside. I was still standing in the same spot, staring at the floor, hoping that a meteor would crash through the ceiling and vaporize me.

"Chase?" Coach Cooper asked as he stepped out of his office. "Why aren't you on the field?"

"I'm not on a team," I replied, trying not to sound devastated. "It's cool though. I can just hang out in here."

The coach shook his head. "Nuh-uh," he hummed. He pointed his thumb over his shoulder toward his office. "You can't stay in here alone. We just got the mascot costume today and it's sitting on my desk. Go put it on and join us out by the field. If you can't play, you can at least run around in that thing."

I wasn't too excited by the idea of wearing a costume, which was ironic because I was wearing my ninja costume under my street clothes at that exact moment. "But really, it's okay if I just—"

"C'mon, son," the coach said as he walked toward the exit.

I shuddered. I hated when anyone, other than my parents, called me son. Walking to Coach Cooper's office, I saw the costume that he was talking about. It was just an oversized mask, gloves, and boots, all covered with brown fur. It looked *hideous!* Who in the world chose *that* to be the mascot? Oh right... it was me.

Defeated, I entered his office and put on the costume.

Five minutes later, I was out on the field wearing the ridiculous moose costume. I felt like I was working at an amusement park. All I needed was a cotton candy cart and a bunch of balloons tied to my wrist.

I stood on the sidelines as everyone else in class played a game of football. Every now and then I waved my hands and did a happy dance because Coach Cooper suggested I do *that* instead of standing completely still. "A moose with a human body that's staring at a bunch of people is the stuff of nightmares," is what he said.

Through the eyeholes in the mask, I watched as Brayden's team did their best to compete against Jake's team. I had no idea why Brayden didn't choose me first or even at all. My ears felt warm as I silently grew angrier under the moose mask.

GROSS, RIGHT?

Suddenly I saw a bunch of kids running straight for me. I stumbled backward, afraid for my life. When I looked up, I could see a football spinning out of control through the air

"Nooo!" I shouted, putting my hands up. The football missed me, but a bunch of kids on Jake's team slammed into my body, forcing me to the ground. The moose mask acted like a helmet, preventing my skull from bouncing against the field.

"Sorry, man," said the kid that tackled me. I recognized him as one of the guys from the wolf pack. He held his hand out to help me up.

And then I saw it – a red band dangling from the kid's wrist. It meant this kid was a red ninja. I didn't want to seem suspicious, so I grabbed his hand and allowed him to help me up.

As I looked at the other two members of the wolf pack, I saw that they were wearing red wristbands as well. Wyatt's ninja clan reached farther than I thought.

"C'mon already!" shouted Jake as he jogged over. He put his hands on his knees and caught his breath. It gave me a clear view of the red band he had around his wrist too. Jake was also a red ninja.

I stared at Jake through my moose mask.

"Hey, mascot," Jake said, straightening his posture. "You see that Chase kid anywhere out here?"

Hesitant, I shook my head. I was afraid of saying anything in case he recognized my voice.

"He must've stayed inside to cry," Jake said, looking over his shoulder at the school.

I shrugged, biting my lip out of anger so I wouldn't explode with rage.

Jake snickered and brought his attention back to me. "I'd suspect *you* were Chase, but there's no way you're a dude under that mask."

"Yeah," one of Jake's friends said. "You move too gracefully while you cheer from the sidelines."

I torqued my head, upset and flattered at the same time. Upset because they just called me a girl, but flattered because moving gracefully *was* a strength for a ninja. I gave them a two-thumbs-up and craned my neck so the mask would look like it was nodding.

"Kay," Jake said as he picked up the football. "If you see Chase, you let us know alright, sweetheart?"

I continued to nod, gritting my teeth the entire time.

Jake and his wolf pack went back to the football game. Brayden's team was clearly on the losing side, but they looked like they were still having fun.

Hopping around like an idiot, I continued to cheer on the football game. As long as I didn't act different, I wasn't worried about anyone figuring out who I was.

Apparently Jake and his wolf pack were red ninjas now, which meant they knew who Wyatt was, which also meant they probably knew I was the leader of my own ninja clan. Things were getting worse at Buchanan. Much worse.

Monday. 11:31 AM. Lunch.

Once gym was over, I changed out of the moose costume as quickly as I could and ran out of the locker room. I had no desire to get confronted by Jake and his wolf pack.

After bolting out into the hallway, I took a hard left turn and sprinted down the hall. Posters of Sophia's missing penguin adorned the brick walls of every corridor I could see.

I was supposed to meet Gavin back in the cafeteria, but I wanted to check on my ninja clan before their training.

The ninja clan I lead used to meet in a secret hideout in the woods during gym class, but because of a series of disastrous events, the hideout was demolished to make room for a new set of bleachers. Since then, we've been meeting in an empty classroom near the back of the school during lunch.

I pretended to start a club called Alien Language Arts. Principal Davis thought it was a pretty cool idea since he's really into sci-fi shows about time traveling doctors or something. He didn't skip a beat, and said I could have the room.

Saying it was to study alien languages pretty much secured the fact that no one would ever try to join it, except for the principal that one time. I had to convince him that it would've been weird for the other students if he sat in on the class. He took off his oversized scarf and walked away, disappointed. I felt awful about it, but secrecy is the most important thing to a ninja clan.

I opened the door that had the Alien Language Arts sign taped to it, and stepped into the room. When I first started at

Buchanan, there were nearly fifty members in the ninja clan, but over the last few months, that number had dropped dramatically. I scanned the area and only counted twenty ninjas. I wasn't sure why kids were quitting, and I knew at some point I'd look into it, but that point hadn't come yet.

"Sir!" shouted one of my more dedicated ninjas. It was a girl named Naomi. She stood before the other ninjas, holding her mask in her hand. Whipping her short brown hair out of her face, she smirked at me. "Good to see you."

The other ninjas in the room stood at attention and thumped their chests once, shouting, "Ha!" at the same time.

I sighed, shutting the door behind me. "Guys, we got a problem," I said.

"The missing penguin?" Naomi asked.

I nodded. "Seems like the penguin isn't even the *real* problem. My buddy thinks the penguin was just a distraction so the real crime could be committed."

"What was the *real* crime?"

"Someone tried busting the stage," I replied, glancing at the clock on the wall. It was already 11:35, and Gavin would probably be waiting outside the cafeteria for me. "I'm sorry, you guys. I gotta run, but if you could all keep an eye on the things happening around the talent show for anything fishy, I'd appreciate it. I know my cousin would too."

"But what about training?" one of the ninjas at the back of the classroom said.

"Naomi can take over for the week," I said.

Naomi smiled at me, punched her open palm and nodded once. The other ninjas behind her did the same.

I walked out of the room feeling a little guilty that I had to spend another training session away from my ninja clan, but I had to shake the feeling off. There was a criminal on the loose, and I had to stop him.

Monday. 11:40 AM. Lunch.

The line for the kitchen was long, so I decided to skip it and head straight into the cafeteria. I knew my stomach was going to hate me later for it, which meant it would probably grumble during the quietest moment in class. I hate when that happens because it guarantees someone will turn around, point at me, and yell, "He farted!" at the top of their lungs.

Gavin was waiting for me just inside the cafeteria. He was standing next to one of the garbage cans, fiddling with a mini notepad in his hands, and scanning the room for anything that might lead us to the kid in the hockey mask.

Along the far wall was the stage that had the collapsed corner. Half-painted banners were drying off on top of it.

Eyeballing the room, I noticed it felt a little emptier than normal. It was still filled with students, but there were pockets of empty tables and spaces. Normally the lunchroom is packed with hardly a place to sit, but at the moment, it felt like half the students were missing.

"Zoe probably still hates me, huh?" I asked, joining Gavin by his side.

Gavin nodded, flipping open his notepad. On the first page, he had scribbled a few notes. At the bottom of the page was a crudely drawn penguin with the name Sophia written after it.

"It looks like the penguin's name is 'Sophia' according to your notes," I joked.

Gavin ignored me as he scanned the room for Sophia.

31

"Since she's an orchestra nerd, she'll probably be sitting with a bunch of her orchestra friends."

"What's *that* supposed to mean?" I asked, offended. I think I was still shaken by what Jake had said to me during gym. "Oh, so because she loves orchestra, she's automatically a nerd?"

"Calm down," Gavin said. "I don't mean it like that."

"How *else* can you mean it?"

"When I say 'nerd,' I mean someone who's really into something, y'know?" Gavin said. "Sophia loves orchestra and is really good at playing cello, which means she probably practices it on her own time. So she's an orchestra nerd. Some kids like sports, right? They play the sport, watch the sport, and talk about the sport 24/7, which makes them a sports nerd. I'm using nerd in a good way here."

Pushing my hands into my front pockets, I sunk my head into my shoulders. "Yeah, I *guess* I know what you're talking about. Still doesn't feel right calling someone a nerd though."

Gavin put his hands up as he continued across the cafeteria. "Sorry, alright? I should've used a different term."

"Fine," I said. "Apology accepted."

On both sides of the aisle, students were burying their faces in their lunches. It was pickled meatloaf day, which for some strange reason, kids at Buchanan went *nuts* over.

As we searched the cafeteria for Sophia, I overhead a few students gossiping.

"Did you hear they still haven't found that penguin?"

"I heard it was a whole team of penguins that got away!"

"Did you know if you feed a penguin after midnight, it'll transform into a little green monster?"

"I think you're thinking of a movie."

"Nope, pretty sure it's real life. Saw a documentary on it."

"Yeah, that was a movie."

"We'll see who's laughing after midnight."

Kids at Buchanan were weird.

Finally, Gavin stopped and pointed ahead. "There she is," he said.

I followed as he stepped up to the table where Sophia sat. Other orchestra students sat with her, looking rather bored. She was wearing thick-rimmed glasses without the lenses in them, along with headphones that weren't hooked up to anything. Everyone at the table was dressed like they were straight out of a 1930's movie about the future, which is the standard style for hipsters.

SOPHIA

Hipsters have a way of making others feel like they're outdated. If anything seems fresh and new, a hipster will always make a remark about how it's lame and boring already, as if they're ahead of the curve. Hipsters make me sick, almost as much as pirates, because you can never *like* anything if a hipster is around.

She glanced at us as she jabbed at her pickled meatloaf. The last part of her conversation was clear as we approached.

"...so yeah," Sophia said to her friends. "That new bow is about three hundred bucks, and I'm totally gonna buy it next week." She stopped as soon as she noticed us. "S'up?" she asked all cool.

Gavin raised his foot and set it on an empty chair. "Funny business this morning with that penguin, ain't it?"

"*Isn't* it," Sophia said, correcting Gavin's grammar. "And

no, it's not funny at all. My penguin is still running around somewhere in this school."

"They haven't found it yet?" I asked.

"No," Sophia replied, her lip quivering. "It breaks my heart to think that Hotcakes is scared and alone right now."

I paused, chocking back a chuckle. "Your penguin's name... is *Hotcakes?*"

"So?" Sophia snipped, annoyed.

"Is it 'cause he likes pancakes or something?" Gavin asked.

"Are you serious?" Sophia replied. "Penguins can't eat pancakes. It's just a cute name."

Gavin put his hands up, surrendering. "Sorry," he said. "If you wouldn't mind, Chase and I would like to ask you a couple questions about this morning and... *Hotcakes.*"

I chocked back another chuckle, putting my fist up to my mouth and coughing. "Excuse me," I said.

Sophia glanced at her orchestra friends at the table and sighed. Her friends all sighed in response, which was a typical hipster thing to do. It was almost like they were telling each other they were bored without actually using words. "Fine, go ahead and ask," Sophia said, waving her hand at Gavin.

Gavin flipped open his notepad and clicked the butt of his pen. "Can you tell us what happened this morning?"

Sophia's eyebrows raised as she took a deep breath. "Well, I got to school early 'cause Zoe said all the acts needed to rehearse or something. I think she was extra excited about the fact that I had a penguin in my act."

"Who *wouldn't* be?" I muttered.

Sophia continued. "So I set Hotcake's cage down by the bench against the wall. I walked away from him for like, a *second*, and then I heard everyone screaming." Sophia's voice cracked as she covered her face.

"It's alright," Gavin said softly. "Take your time."

"I'm just so worried about him," Sophia sniffled. "He was supposed to be back by now!"

"Yeah, we thought the school would've caught him by now too," Gavin said.

Sophia paused, making a long face while she carefully wiped the tears away from under her eyes.

"Did you see who might've opened the cage?" I asked.

Through her sobbing, she mumbled something hard to understand. "I don't know, *I* just... *it* just... Eli said... I mean, I think I saw... I dunno, okay? It all happened so *fast!*"

Gavin scribbled Eli's name onto his notepad. "Did you just say Eli?"

Sophia took another deep breath. "Yeah, I mean, no. I meant to say *Calvin.* I'm pretty sure I saw Calvin messing around with Hotcakes before everything happened."

"Calvin," Gavin repeated, adding the name to his notes.

Sophia suddenly frowned as she leaned her head over. "Can we be done, please? I don't want to talk about this anymore. I just want to find Hotcakes and make sure he's safe."

Nodding, Gavin spoke. "Thank you for your time, and if you hear anything, please let us know."

"What are you, like, the Buchanan detective team or something?" she asked.

In my mind, I couldn't help but imagine what our logo

would look like if Gavin and I *did* form a detective team.

Gavin laughed. "Nah, we just want to help Zoe get this talent show back on track, and also to make sure that Hotcakes doesn't get hurt."

"Thank you for that," Sophia said, smiling through the mascara running down her cheeks. "Thank you."

Gavin nodded, flipped his notepad shut, and started walking down the aisle. I followed behind him, glancing at the corners of the cafeteria. Hotcakes had been set free just that morning, so he couldn't have gotten far. I wasn't sure how many exits there were to the cafeteria, but I doubted there were a lot.

"At least we got a name," Gavin said.

"Calvin," I said. "Since I'm pretty new at this school, I don't recognize the name. Do you know him?"

"Surprisingly I don't," Gavin admitted. "I thought I knew everyone here, but I guess I was wrong."

"Could he be a new student?" I asked.

Gavin raised his eyebrows. "Possibly, but I'd be surprised if there was a new kid that I didn't hear about."

"Maybe he's *that* new?"

Gavin stopped at the cafeteria doors. "Maybe. We'll have to ask around some more, but in the meantime, Sophia also mentioned Eli. He's someone I *do* know."

"But she *meant* to say Calvin," I said.

"Since we don't know anyone by the name of Calvin, then I say we start with the first name she gave us," Gavin said. "It won't hurt our investigation, and maybe he'll even know who this Calvin kid is."

I couldn't argue with him. "Makes sense," I said. "So where's Eli at?"

Gavin sighed as he glanced at the clock on the wall. "We'll have to wait until tomorrow to ask him anything. I looked for him while we were walking out of the cafeteria, but couldn't find him. That's okay though. It'll give us time to collect our thoughts." Gavin clutched his hands on his stomach. "Plus I'm *starving.*"

I smiled at the thought of food. We spent the rest of lunch eating nasty pickled meatloaf and arguing who would win in a battle between cowboys and ninjas.

Tuesday. 7:45 AM. The cafeteria.

My dad brought me to school early again so I could help Zoe in the cafeteria. She didn't ask for my help, but I figured that showing up was better than *not* showing up. The few times I called her cell phone the night before, I could tell she hit the ignore button because it rang once and sent me directly to her voicemail.

As I walked through the halls, I saw photocopies of the missing penguin hanging from the brick walls. The words, "Have you seen me?" were printed in bold font underneath the picture.

Finally, I arrived at the cafeteria. Through the tinted glass windows, I watched as the silhouettes of students moved back and forth within the room, setting up more random stuff for the talent show. I pushed the doors open, and stepped inside.

I had missed out on helping the day before so I never got a chance to see everyone working together. I have to admit – the sight was incredible.

Several kids were on the far side of the room finishing up the banners that would be hung later in the day. They were huge – at least eight feet wide and four feet tall.

Gavin and some other guys were fixing up the broken section of the stage. He shouted a couple of orders at the guys on the other end of the platform, telling them to lift their side higher so he could slip some books under his corner.

At random parts of the room were students working on whatever task Zoe had assigned for them. Some were playing with the colored spotlights, switching them on and off with the controls at the back of the room.

A few kids were sitting near a table with the soundboard on top of it. Every couple of seconds, they would turn the knobs on the soundboard and check the microphones to see what the knob did.

The rest of the students were a whirlwind of activity, running back and forth across the room, trying to set up various pieces of material for specific acts. It looked like the next act that was going to test the sound was a band because some kids were carrying pieces of a drum set across the cafeteria.

On the other side of the room was the long bench I had seen the previous morning. After seeing it for a second time, it was a little more obvious that it was the spot where students waited their turn to perform. The bench was against the far wall that led to the backstage. Just above the bench was the metal scaffolding with paint cans still sitting on top of it.

Zoe was a few feet away from me, staring at a clipboard. She was wearing a yellow construction hat and shouting orders into a walkie-talkie.

"We've only got four days until the show," Zoe barked. "And you're only telling me *now* that we've got a problem with the pyrotechnics?"

Pyrotechnics? Like, fireworks and stuff? Man, my cousin could be pretty cool sometimes. She was planning on putting on the most epic talent show in history!

"Zoe?" I said as I walked up to her.

Zoe turned around, but didn't smile. "Chase," she said, and then returned her attention to the walkie-talkie. "I don't care *how* you figure it out, but *figure* it out! No more excuses!"

"Who's on the other end of that conversation?" I asked.

Zoe pressed her lips together and rolled her eyes. "Principal Davis."

"No way!" I said. "You didn't just *command* the principal to do something, did you?"

She set her walkie-talkie on a table nearby. "One of our acts has a pyrotechnic display, nothing huge, just some loud pops and sparklers, but we can't test anything until the inspector comes in and says we can. The problem is that the inspector is out of town for the week, so the principal has to figure out another way to get our pyro approved."

I gotta hand it to Zoe – if she wanted something done, she figured out how to get it done. I shuffled my feet a bit, embarrassed. "Look, I'm sorry about last weekend. I should've been here to help."

Zoe's eyes looked at me from under the construction helmet. "Go on..."

"But I'm here now," I continued. "And I'm willing to do whatever I can to make things right even if it means picking up a hammer and getting my hands dirty."

"Don't you live by some ninja code or something?" my cousin asked. "Wouldn't it have been the honorable thing for you to help family if they asked for it."

"Yes, you're right," I said, "which is why I said *should've* helped you."

Zoe folded her arms. "It shouldn't take a ninja code for you to understand how to be there for someone else... especially if that 'someone else' is family."

I tilted my head back, tired of getting scolded. "Come onnnn! You know I'm sorry! You know I'm a good kid at heart! Here's a list of awesome things I've done since yesterday." I held my palm out and extended a finger for everything in my list. "I fed some stray cats. I helped an old lady find her car keys – it doesn't matter that she was my mom, it still counts! I held the door open for some cute girls. I let that Davian kid borrow my mechanical pencil even though I fully knew he wasn't going to give it back! I ate *all* of my vegetables last night for dinner, and *you know* that vegetables are one of my worst enemies! I *didn't* get into an argument with the comic shop salesperson about how ninjas *wouldn't* stand a chance in a zombie apocalypse because he *clearly* wasn't thinking straight since his parents kicked him out of their basement! And I showed up to school early today so I could help you!"

Zoe furrowed her brow. "A real hero doesn't need to take credit for every good thing they do. That makes you sound like you're doing good things because you want people to say how great you are."

"Fiiiiiine," I whined. "I'm sorry!"

"Your apology won't mean a darn thing to me if you get all huffy puffy right now," Zoe said.

"Okay," I replied, hanging my head low. I couldn't help but smile. "You're right, okay? Happy? I *should've* helped you and I was a butthead for telling you no."

Zoe wagged her finger at me. "It wasn't that you told me 'no.' If you would've just said 'no,' then I wouldn't have cared. It's that you told me you didn't want your *nap* to get interrupted!"

I chuckled. "Yes, you're right about that too."

"Is that funny to you?" Zoe asked, glaring at me.

I paused, but decided to be honest. "C'mon, it's a *little* funny."

Zoe stared at me for another second. Her eyes looked cold and mechanical, but suddenly she LOL'd. "Fine," she said, coughing through her laugh. "It might be a *little* funny."

I set my book bag on the table next to us and scanned the room. "Is there anything I can do to help right now?"

Zoe picked up her clipboard and read through her notes, silently moving her head back and forth with each new line on her task sheet. "I think Gavin still needs some help—"

"Wait," I said, interrupting my cousin. Something had caught my eye at the far corner of the cafeteria. It moved so quickly that it was a black and white blur.

Zoe set her clipboard down. "What is it?"

And then I saw it. The penguin had hopped down from the stage and stood out in the open. It was Hotcakes.

I acted instantly, ignoring Zoe's question. My body went from zero to sixty in about three seconds as I sprinted across the room.

"Chase!" I heard Zoe shout. "*What* are you doing?"

The penguin snapped its attention at me as I ran toward it. Spinning around, it started waddling to the long bench with the scaffolding above it. I don't know what you've heard about penguins, but those little birds are *fast*. Faster than I'd ever imagined, at least.

The gasps of other students floated past me as I ran faster for the loose bird. I could hear Gavin shout something from behind me, but I couldn't tell what it was. I was too focused on catching the penguin.

The black and white bird dashed along the wall, flipping its pointless wings in the air. I responded smoothly, cutting a curve across the middle of the room. That bird wasn't going to get away again if I had anything to do with it!

The penguin made it to the long bench under the scaffolding, hopping onto it in one bounce. Racing across the cafeteria, I watched as it jumped onto one of the metal rungs of the scaffolding. And then it slipped, falling against the wooden bench and flopping to the floor. It jumped back to its feet and started waddling again.

"Don't you move!" I shouted at the penguin.

I was only about five feet away when I dropped to my side and slid along the ground like I was sliding for first base. The penguin stopped in its tracks and faced me. Opening its beak wide, it screamed like a banshee. I'm not embarrassed to say it freaked me out enough that I broke from my controlled slide, kicking my feet along the polished floor and covering my face from the penguin.

I felt my body smash into the long wooden bench, finally stopping me. The scaffolding above the bench tilted back and forth until the wooden plank at the top flipped to its side. All the materials that were on the board crashed to the floor next to me. Paintbrushes and rollers bounced around me. A heavily braided rope swung back and forth from the scaffolding to a dark spot backstage where it disappeared. The only reason I noticed the rope was because it had pink and green threads sewn into it.

My eyes followed the rope from the backstage all the way to the plank where it was tied to one of the corners. Thankfully, the plank itself didn't fall off, the same way it hadn't fallen off the day before. I rolled to my stomach, staring across the floor. There was no sign of the penguin.

I saw Zoe staring at me. Gavin was laughing right behind her. Defeated, I dropped my head and felt it bump against the cold floor.

"Ya done?" Gavin's voice asked. His shoes stepped into my field of vision, blocking my view of the rest of the cafeteria.

"Is it gone?" I asked behind my palms.

Gavin took a knee on the floor. "That thing was gone before you hit the bench. It ran right back into the air vent."

"Chase! OMG, are you okay?" Faith asked as she jogged up to me.

"I'm fine," I said, rising from the floor. "I'm just upset the penguin got away."

Zoe approached, looking upset. "Nice one," she snipped, pointing at the broken painting materials on the floor. "You seem to make a mess of things everywhere you go, don't you?"

Here I thought she was going to praise me for trying to catch the penguin. I took a breath, annoyed that she wasn't happy with me yet again, but I kept my mouth shut. Anything I said would've only made things worse. Instead, I stared at the plank of wood that had tipped over on top of the scaffolding.

Zoe marched away and shouted some more orders into her walkie-talkie about how there was another accident that needed fixing in the cafeteria. Faith smiled at me, letting me know that she wasn't mad. Gavin stood in place, staring at the air vent the penguin had used to escape.

My eyes drifted across the broken painting supplies as I nudged them with my foot. Looking back at the plank, I noticed the paint cans on the end of it. I don't know how I didn't notice it before, but they were all tipped sideways too, still attached to the wooden board with the braided rope dangling off the side. Wow. Thank goodness those paint cans hadn't fallen or else this whole thing would've been much worse.

I studied the cans of paint closer and noticed that they had been secured to the wooden plank with nails all along their bases. Several paint cans had been attached to the wood.

But why would anyone nail paint cans into wood?

Stepping to the end of the plank, I grabbed the handle to one of the cans and pulled, but the thing didn't budge. My fingers slipped and the handle popped back into place.

"What in the..." I whispered.

Gavin heard me. "What's the matter?"

Tapping the plank, I spoke. "These cans are nailed to the wood."

Gavin reached up and slid his finger along the base of one of the cans. "Man, you're one lucky duck," he said. "If these cans had been open, I'm pretty sure Zoe would never speak to you again."

"That's weird, right?" I asked, unsure of the answer myself.

"Sure is," Gavin said, turning toward me, and then he changed the subject. "Bell's about to ring. Meet before lunch? We have to ask Eli about yesterday still."

"Sure," I said, glancing at the clock just in time to see it click and hear the bell ring.

Gavin walked to the door, but before he left the cafeteria, he turned and said one last thing. "Eli won't be in the cafeteria though. He's one of those straight A students who use that time to work in the library so we'll have to look in there today. Grab Brayden before we go."

"Brayden?" I asked. "Why?"

"He's a monster expert, right?"

I nodded.

Gavin smiled. "Library's fulla zombies. We'll need his help for this one."

I stood still in the middle of the cafeteria as students left the room. I think my ears were trying to convince my brain that I had actually heard Gavin correctly.

Did that kid really just say something about zombies?

Tuesday. 10:50 AM. Gym class.

I stood on the sidelines in gym class just as I had the day before. Coach Cooper said that the teams had been picked for the entire week so I was going to be stuck with the ridiculous moose costume for the next few days. You'd think he'd rotate another student out so that I could get in a game or two, but he never said anything about that. He just sat near the entrance of the gymnasium, sipping his half lemonade, half tea mixture.

I guess I couldn't complain too much. Keeping me in the mascot costume was a good way to stay out of trouble since apparently, trouble was looking for me.

"Anyone see that dweeb, Chase?" Jake hollered from the football field.

Several kids shook their heads. Brayden made sure to keep his eyes on the field rather than risk giving me away by sneaking a peek at me. I heard a few others comment on the fact that they had no idea anyone in their gym class even had the name "Chase."

Jake put his hands on his hips and searched the members of both teams. I was standing next to the football field, dancing the way I'd expect a professional mascot to dance – like a dork.

"That kid's so afraid of you that he's not even coming out to the field!" one of the boy's in Jake's wolf pack said.

"It's not his fault," Jake replied. "He's just afraid of sports since he's a *nerdling.*"

Jake laughed at his own joke. His wolf pack took that as their sign to laugh too.

Once the game got started, it was easier for me to chill a little. After a few touchdowns from Jake's team, they were so satisfied with the lead that they stopped asking about where I was.

After an embarrassing turnover, Brayden's team had the ball. I'll admit that I'm not much of a sports guy, but I at least knew when a team was winning or losing, and at that moment, I knew Brayden's team was losing. Bad.

I watched as a short kid on Brayden's team hiked the ball. The QB snatched it and took a few steps back, searching for someone, anyone, to throw it to. I heard Brayden's voice come from down the field and I looked over to see that he was completely out in the open.

Turning my huge mascot head, I started jumping up and down, pointing at Brayden. The QB chucked the ball so hard that it wobbled through the air. Time seemed to stand still as I watched the ball float through space until finally...

Jake jumped through the air like some kind of lion going after its prey. Snatching the ball with one hand, he sailed into Brayden, smashing against him. Brayden looked like a ragdoll as he fell to the ground. I could see the pain in his face.

Jake jogged back to his goal line and into the end zone, scoring another six points for his team. His wolf pack ran circles around Brayden, laughing and making fun of him the entire time while he sat on the ground, rubbing his hurt knees.

It was awful, and I was starting to feel my anger swell up from deep within my stomach, but I knew I couldn't do anything without starting *some* type of scuffle.

Jake danced in the end zone for what seemed like an hour. He kept pointing two fingers in the air as he tapped his knees together over and over and over... and over.

I jogged to the end of the field, behind the goal post, and watched Brayden as his team helped him up. A few kids from my ninja clan were on his team so it was good to see that they were by his side too.

After a moment, Jake's team set up for the kickoff as Brayden's team took their place at the other end of the field. A tall boy from the wolf pack ran at full speed toward the football, and then did that little rapid step move to make sure they had enough room. He booted the ball so hard it flew all the way across the field, past the fifty-yard line, past Brayden's team, past the goal post…

…and directly at me.

I froze, watching as the brown ball came closer and closer. My normal response to an inflated leather ball, coming at me at a hundred miles an hour, was to flinch and dive to the ground, but for some reason I didn't do that. Instead, I held my arms out, catching the ball perfectly with the hairy moose gloves on my hands.

"Go!" Brayden cried.

I looked up, through the eyeholes in my mask. All I could hear was my breath as it turned into quick gasps inside the mask. It sounds like it might've been cool, but it actually seemed like something out of a scary movie.

I didn't have to think about it anymore because for some reason my legs starting booking it. I guess they decided they were going to try and score a touchdown.

"Get him!" Jake shouted from the other end of the field. "*Get that moose!*"

So there I was – a kid in an oversized moose mask running straight into a team of students who wanted to tackle me. If you could see the play from overhead, you'd see a tiny dot running into a bunch of other tiny dots.

Members of Jake's wolf pack were close enough that I could smell their cheap cologne. I wanted to brace for impact, but my legs had something else in mind.

Something *ninja.*

As soon as the first kid dove at me, I jumped into the air, spinning around so I faced the opposite direction. Sailing over his head, I laughed as I completed the turn, landing on my feet at full speed. I clutched the ball closer to my side and leaned into my sprint. Oh yeah, this was going to be *fun.*

Two other kids ran right at me. The first one dove, but before he caught me, I dug my foot into the dirt and spun a circle clean around him. The other boy reached his arms out. I felt his fingers slide against the moose mask so I dipped my head down, slipping free from his grip, spinning circles like crazy, trying to confuse him. I didn't have to worry about him after that. He fell face first into the ground.

I steadied myself as the world spun outside my moose mask. I had to keep running. If I stopped long enough, someone from Jake's team was sure to tackle me.

Feeling a little sick to my stomach, I continued to run as fast as I could toward the end zone. Most of the kids on Jake's team had stopped running after me, allowing me to pass by with almost no effort at all. It was like they had given up because I was too fast for them!

"Stop him!" I heard another voice shout.

I took that as my hint to run even faster so I obeyed. My legs burned as I pushed myself harder to score a touchdown for Brayden's team. Sneaking a glance to my left, I could see the lines in the football field counting down as a sportscaster shouted in my mind.

"He's at the forty! The thirty! The twenty! The ten!"

And then Brayden's voice slipped into the mask. *"You're going the wrong way!"*

I looked over my shoulder to see Brayden and his team gazing at me as if I were crazy. Jake and his team were clear on the other side of the field, laughing. I tried to stop, but it was impossible because of how fast I was going.

"Touchdown!" Jake shouted from across the field.

I slowed to a stop, letting the football drop into the grass.

At that moment, Coach Cooper's bear horn went off, signaling for all the students to return to the locker rooms to get changed.

"Nice," Brayden said.

I didn't say anything, too embarrassed to defend myself.

Our classmates all ran past us, desperate to change out of their gym clothes. Jake and his wolf pack laughed at me when they walked by. If they knew who it was under the mask, I'm sure their taunting would've been harsher. Brayden and I were the last ones on the field.

As soon as Jake was in the gym, I took off my mask. "Dude, I'm sorry about that."

Brayden squinted his eyes, looking at the sky.

I wasn't sure if he was angry or sad. "Dude?"

Suddenly, he burst out laughing. Wiping the tears from his eyes, he spoke through quick gasps. "You totally scored for the wrong team! I thought that sort of thing only happened in movies!"

I smiled, relieved. "I guess not," I said, chuckling.

"No," Brayden said. "You *really* biffed it out there! Like, it was going awesome and cool up until you spun around in a million circles!"

I scratched the back of my neck. "Yeah, not sure what I was thinking with that one."

Brayden continued to laugh. "And then you started running straight back to where you came from! And like, running *harder* than you were before! You were *determined* to score that touchdown!"

I started feeling a little stupid. "Yeah, funny," I said, biting my lip.

"Sorry, man," Brayden said, smearing his hand across his tear soaked cheek. "I mean, that was just the funniest thing I'd seen all year. My *cheeks* hurt! Thanks for the laugh."

I put my hand on his shoulder and squeezed. "No problem, man."

Brayden stretched his arms out and sighed, finally able to catch his breath. "So what's up?" he asked as he headed back toward the locker rooms.

Walking next to him, I remembered what Gavin had said earlier. "Actually, Gavin said he needs your help, well, *we* need your help."

"Anything for my ninja leader," Brayden said jokingly.

"We have a lead on a suspect," I said. "Someone named Eli that might know something about the broken stage yesterday."

"Okay," Brayden said, nodding.

I continued. "Gavin said he's a straight A student so he'll in the library during lunch, studying or something. So I guess you'll need to meet us outside the cafeteria before lunch starts."

Brayden stopped in place. "Free period in the library during lunch?" he whispered.

"Yeah," I said. "The same thing Zoe does sometimes I guess."

"*Zombies*," Brayden whispered.

I paused, surprised at what my best friend had said. "Gavin said the same thing!"

Brayden nodded, his eyes peeled open, staring at me. "He's right," he said, jogging away from me. "You guys are gonna need my help!"

My body sunk as I put my arms out. "Really? You're just gonna say '*zombies*,' and then run off with no explanation whatsoever?"

Brayden didn't turn around. Once he made it to the gymnasium entrance, he pulled open the door and jumped inside.

Pulling the moose gloves off my hands, I stuffed them into the mask and kept trudging back to the school. Lunch was coming up shortly so whatever crazy thing Gavin and Brayden were talking about, would be cleared up soon.

There was no way Buchanan School had zombies walking around, right? This was real life, and zombies only existed in movies and video games, didn't they? I suddenly realized I was trying to convince myself that they didn't exist because in that moment, I wasn't too sure.

Tuesday. 11:30 AM. Lunch.

Before finding Gavin and Brayden, I thought I'd pay my ninja clan another visit. All the talk of zombies in the library had me a little on edge, so I wanted to refocus my thoughts on something more realistic. But of course, Buchanan School had something *else* in mind for me.

As I turned the corner in the hallway, I saw a crowd of kids standing outside the room my ninja clan used for training. When I got closer, I realized the crowd *was* my ninja clan. They were standing in the middle of the hall, grumbling about something.

"Hey, guys," I said. "What gives? How come you're out here and in your street clothes still?"

Naomi pointed at the door. "Because of *him*."

A lump formed in my throat as I looked through the rectangular section of glass on the door. Right on the other side of the entrance was Wyatt and another girl.

Suddenly the door whipped open, and Wyatt flinched, acting surprised that we were in the hallway. "Oh, excuse me," he said unpleasantly. "Had no idea anyone was out here."

"What're you doing with this room?" I snipped.

"This?" Wyatt asked, turning in a circle. "Oh I saw that the school had an empty room so decided it'd be a great place to train my... *hall monitors*."

"That's *bologna*, and you know it," I shouted, angry. I made sure to pronounce "bologna" incorrectly, enunciating the "*g*," so it sounded like "bah-*log*-na!"

52

Suddenly, a girl stepped into view and stood at Wyatt's side, holding his hand. It was Olivia Jones, the girl who tried to destroy the science fair two weeks ago. She smiled smugly as she gnawed on a bright green piece of gum. The air was filled with a spearmint scented evil.

"Trouble, babe?" Olive asked Wyatt.

I coughed. "*Babe?*"

"You haven't heard?" Wyatt asked. "Olive and I are going out now."

"I'm in '*like*' with him," Olive said.

"Gross," I whispered, noticing the red band on her wrist.

Olive saw what I was looking at and lifted her hand to show off her new bracelet. "Like it? I earned it two weeks ago when Wyatt found out that it was *I* who tried to sabotage the science fair."

Wyatt grinned. "Looks like she's the first lady, *and* a red ninja."

"The first lady?" Naomi asked. "But how? Don't you need

to be the president's wife to have that position?"

Wyatt explained. "The rules say if the president isn't married, which Sebastian being a sixth grader obviously *isn't*, then the position of first lady goes to his niece. James Buchanan, the fifteenth president of the United States was in the same situation. His niece acted as the first lady." Wyatt lowered his gaze and gave us the best angry eyes he could. "Now get lost before I send you all to the principal's office. If you remember, I'm the captain of the hall monitors."

Naomi snapped. She balled her fists and held them out to Wyatt. "That does it! This ends here and now!"

Wyatt stepped in front of Olive and held his open palm out as if he were inviting someone to fight him. His face was cool and collected, which made him more eerie.

I had to push against the rest of my ninja clan as they tried moving forward. Grabbing Naomi's elbow, I did my best to remain calm. "No! *Not* like this! This is *exactly* what he wants!"

"Then I say let's give it to him!" Naomi said, pulling my arm free from my grasp. "It's not like he doesn't deserve it!"

"It's not our place to decide what he deserves and what he doesn't!" I said, surprised at my own insight. "The first rule of our ninja clan is that we *don't* fight! Have you all forgotten this?"

"Then what's the point of being in a ninja clan?" Wyatt laughed.

"*Honor*," I said immediately. "Doing the right thing. And at this moment, it's clear that the right thing is to walk away... even if I don't want to."

Wyatt pointed down the hall. "So go already! Get lost 'cause you're a bunch of losers on the *losing* side."

I had to bite my lip to keep from saying anything else. I stared at Wyatt for a few more seconds, angry as heck, but I finally made myself take a breath. Honestly, I felt the same way as the rest of the kids in my ninja clan. But I was their leader, and I had to act as one even if it meant feeling defeated in doing the right thing, which is actually the opposite of the truth. My victory came from doing the *right* thing, so why did I feel so bad about it?

I swallowed my pride and walked away. My ninja clan stayed in place for a few seconds, but eventually followed me down the hall. Wyatt and Olive remained in the hallway in front of the open door. I'm sure that as soon as the hall was clear, the red ninjas would come out to train in that room.

"We're without a home once again," Naomi grunted with her arms folded.

I turned the corner and saw Gavin and Brayden standing in the lobby, waiting for me. Glancing at Naomi, I spoke. "We are, but it's not the first time this has happened. I'm sure we'll bounce back, but for now, I've got some other business to attend to. Take a break today, alright? Get some lunch, drink some OJ, eat a cookie, and laugh a little. It's not the end of the world."

Naomi smiled and nodded. The rest of my ninja clan chuckled a little too. Things were bad, but we've been through worse, and I was positive that this little speed bump wasn't going to stop us from finding a place to train.

Tuesday. 11:40 AM. The library.

I met with Gavin and Brayden in the lobby. They were in the middle of a conversion about the best way to deal with the library situation. Brayden had the idea of taking it slow so nobody would notice us. Gavin thought running at full speed was a better idea. I still had no idea what they were talking about.

"Okay," I said, leaning against the tinted glass walls of the cafeteria. "Zombies. Explain it. *Now.*"

Gavin paused, darting his eyes at Brayden. "You want to explain this, mister monster expert?"

Brayden didn't hesitate. "Gladly," he said, gesturing toward the library with his hands. "The kids in there are Buchanan's best of the best. They're the straight A students, and as most people know, straight A students are allowed to use their lunch to study in the library if they want to."

"Right," I said, nodding. "So?"

"Let me finish," Brayden said, holding his hand up. "The school is under the assumption that the smart kids will use their free period in the library to further their education by doing some additional studying or research in any area they choose to. It's a great idea in theory because it would allow those kids to finish their homework early and also provide the tools for them to do so, such as books and the Internet."

I nodded, trying to keep up, but it was difficult. Brayden was speaking so fast and he sounded like some kind of college professor. "So what about the zombies?"

Brayden smiled. "The school has given these children unlimited access to Buchanan's Wi-Fi Internet during this free period. They're allowed to use the Internet for any kind of research they need, and if they have smart phones, they're allowed to use their phone's web browser too."

"So what?" I asked, still confused.

"So," Gavin said, interrupting. "Those kids in there ain't usin' the internet for research! They're usin' it to update their statuses and send text messages!"

Brayden put his hand on the library door. "They're brainless zombies, staring at their cell phones. All of them."

"That's *not* a zombie," I said, relieved about the fact that there weren't actually undead monsters in the library.

GAVIN   ME   BRAYDEN

Brayden pulled the door open. "We'll see," he said, stepping in. "Stay close, and keep your mouth shut."

I let Gavin go in front of me so I was the last in line. The cold air from the library hit me like a wall. The rest of the school was heated during the colder months of the year, but for some reason, the library had its air conditioning cranked at full blast. The other thing that surprised me was how abnormally silent the area was.

On the wall to the side of us were the typical motivational posters with kittens hanging onto clotheslines, and shadows of people reading books. I saw more posters of Hotcakes too.

Gavin took the lead and whispered. "Eli will probably be somewhere in the back."

"How do you know?" I asked.

"Zoe said she's seen him in here a few times," Gavin replied. "She noticed because she's the only kid whose eyes aren't glued to her cell."

"I'm not surprised," I said.

More of Buchanan's library came into view as the three of us walked farther. It was a two-story library with an exposed staircase at the center of the room. Surrounding the staircase were several rectangular tables, each with a student seated on one of its four sides, which meant there were four kids to a table.

The lighting in the massive room was different from anywhere else in the school. Instead of harsh fluorescent lights along the ceiling, there were soft yellow lights, casting the room in a warm glow.

And then I finally understood what Brayden had meant when he said that kids were zombies. Every kid in the room was breathing through their mouth and staring into a cell phone they held with both hands about two inches from their face. The sudden sound of clicking buttons was apparent when I realized all their thumbs were frantically typing text messages.

You know how when you walk outside at night and all you hear are the sound of crickets? Well, the room was a lot like that, but instead of cricket chirps, it was the sound of short vibration alerts and random *"ting!"* noises.

Brayden inched his way forward. "Don't make any sudden movements," he whispered. "If you do, then they'll see you."

"What happens if they see us?" I asked.

"You don't want to know," he replied.

As we walked down the aisle, I could see the faces of the zombies seated at their desks. Their skin glowed from their cell phone screens as they continued to breath from their mouths. I had to smile because it looked a lot like the video game aisle in a store where kids were allowed to play a demo. Next time you're at one of those stores, check out that aisle and you'll see what I mean. Every single person playing the game has their neck craned backward and their mouth dropped open as they stare at the television screen, playing a game demo.

Just as we were at the staircase, my foot nudged one of the desk legs. It wasn't hard, but it was enough to cause the four zombies seated at the table to look away from their phones.

"Dude, are you nuts?" Brayden whispered harshly, but it was too late. The zombies had already seen us.

"*Whuuuuuuuut...*" one of the zombies groaned. She flopped her hand on the table until she found her cell phone again. She held it in the air and pointed the screen at me. She had been watching a video of a kitten that was trying to jump out of a box. "*Waaaaaaatch this cuuuuuute videeeeeeoooooo.*"

"Dude, run!" Brayden shouted.

At that instant, every zombie in the room looked up from the phones, squinting so their eyes could adjust. With open mouths, they all started groaning about how we needed to watch whatever cute animal video was on the phone.

Gavin took off, sliding over one of the tables. "C'mon, Chase!"

I didn't waste any time, rolling across the surface of the

same table. The zombies at the desk pointed their phones at me, grumbling about their status updates. I kept my eyes focused on the lights in the ceiling, trying not to catch of glimpse of one of those kitten videos. I'm a ninja at heart, but what kid *wouldn't* want to watch a cute video like that?

The zombies stood from their tables and hobbled in our direction. Their legs must've fallen asleep because they were clumsy, trying to keep their balance and stumbling into each other without bending their knees.

"Eli's back here!" Gavin said, jogging between the tall bookshelves. He paused, looking past me. "Where's Brayden?"

I stopped running and spun in place. The zombies weren't following us, and I could see why. They were all gathering around Brayden as he covered his eyes.

"Go on without me!" Brayden cried. "I'll be fine! I'm done for! The videos! They're too cute to pass up! Go! I'll find you after lunch! *Gooooooooooooooo!*" his voice trailed off. The last thing I heard him say was, "*That kitty's never gonna fit in that tube! Cute little kitty!"*

Brayden had become a zombie. I mean, y'know... at least until *after* lunch.

Gavin finally made it to one of the rooms in the back. Along the wall was a series of doors about six feet apart from each other. Each led to a small study room with a desk and a power outlet. There was a student inside each room. Eli was in the last one.

Before we went in, I peered through the glass door and saw the screen on his phone. It looked like he was shopping for one of those oversized magician's hats – the kind where a bunny goes in, but doesn't come out.

Gavin swung the door open and stepped inside. Eli looked up from his cell phone and flinched, scooting his chair back until it bumped his desk, but with Gavin and I blocking his exit, he was completely trapped.

Eli was dressed as a goth, wearing all black clothing and eyeliner, or *guy-liner* as it's called when a boy wears it. His long greasy hair fell in front of his face as he stared through it. His long sleeved black shirt covered his palms and his black jeans were baggy enough that three people could've easily fit inside them. A couple drops of orange paint were splattered at the bottom of his jeans.

"You seem a tad jumpy," Gavin said with his Texan accent.

"Maybe because you two barged into my study room," Eli said, pushing his long black hair behind his ears.

Gavin started with the questions. "What do you know about yesterday's accident in the cafeteria?"

"I wasn't in lunch yesterday," Eli said, angry. "I'm always in here during lunch."

"Not at lunch," Gavin said. "Yesterday *morning*, when Sophia's penguin was set free."

"Oh that," Eli whispered. After a second, he said, "I know that it was *awesome*, and frankly, I'm *glad* the penguin escaped from his caged life! No animal should have to live like a prisoner."

"Interesting perspective," Gavin said. "So you actually think it's a *good* thing that Hotcakes got loose."

Eli snickered. "Who names a penguin Hotcakes?"

Gavin ignored the question. I assumed that because of Eli's attitude, Gavin was going to treat him like a suspect. "Rumor has it you were around the cage," Gavin said.

"*Everyone* was around that cage," Eli laughed. "It was a *penguin* in a cage! Who *wouldn't* want to see that thing?"

I watched as Gavin stuck his tongue out the side of his mouth and scratched more notes onto his notepad.

Finally, Eli broke the awkward silence. "Oh wait, I get it. You think *I* did it? Well, you're completely wrong about that, *good sirs*. I didn't have anything to do with the penguin or anything else for that matter!"

I folded my arms. "Is there any information you could tell us that might help us find the kid who did it? What did you see yesterday?"

Eli mocked me, folding his arms and leaning back in his chair. "I already told you I didn't do it so we're done here."

Gavin sighed. "What about the kid in the hockey mask? Play any games of hockey recently, Eli? Hmm?"

"If by hockey, you mean hacky sack, then yeah, I've been playing a ton of hacky sack recently," Eli said.

"No," Gavin said, rubbing his eyebrows. "That's *not* what I meant."

Eli continued. "Are you guys, like, the detectives in the

school now? You can't just bust into my study period and demand answers from me, y'know. I have my rights and I want to speak to the principal."

Gavin held his open palms out. "Easy now, cupcake. I just wanted—"

"*Don't* call me *cupcake*," Eli said.

Gavin took a breath.

Eli slid forward on his chair, looking uneasy. "Fine, look, I saw some kid hanging around Sophia's pet bird yesterday morning, alright?"

"Why didn't you say something to begin with?" Gavin asked, straightening his posture, scribbling again on his notepad.

Eli ran his fingers through his hair. "I don't know," he said with a high-pitched voice. "Maybe it's 'cause you two spooked me or something. Anyways, I think the kid you want to ask is Calvin. I saw him poking around that cage yesterday morning."

Gavin wrote the name into his notepad and circled it. "Sophia said something about him too."

"There ya go," Eli said, sitting back. "Find *that* guy."

"But who is he?" I asked. "I've never heard of him before."

Eli's eyes darted at me. "Who are *you*?" he asked with an attitude. "I've been going to this school since kindergarten, and I've never seen *you* before. Just 'cause you haven't seen someone doesn't mean they aren't real. You think the school revolves around you or something?"

Ouch. I lowered my gaze, embarrassed.

"Alright, alright," Gavin said. "So where exactly did you see Calvin?"

Eli shook his head and blinked slowly. "I dunno, backstage I guess? I mean *I* was backstage, I think? I don't know. Everything was pretty crazy when it all went down. Actually, I think I was over by the bench against the wall."

"That's where the penguin was," I said.

"Was it?" Eli asked, confused and scratching his arm. "That's right, I *was* back by the stage. I was checking out some of the backdrops that were being painted."

"Painting?" I asked. "Were *you* painting?"

"No," Eli replied. "Why?"

I almost explained the paint cans that had been nailed to the scaffold. "No reason. I just uh…" I pointed at his jeans. "I just noticed some orange paint on your jeans."

"Oh, dude!" Eli said, rolling his eyes. "My mom's gonna kill me for getting paint on these!"

"Maybe watch where you step next time, huh?" I laughed.

At that moment, the bell rang, signaling the end of lunch. The zombies in the library all shook their heads, returning to normal. Eli snatched his book bag off the floor and hoisted it onto his back.

"See ya, guys," Eli grunted. "This conversation is over. If you come near me again, I swear I'll go straight to Principal Davis and tell him you were messing with me."

Gavin stepped aside from the door. "Thank you for your time," he said politely.

I watched as Eli walked away. When he was gone, I turned back to Gavin. "So he's innocent?" I sighed. "This investigation is beginning to be one dead end after another."

"Not true," Gavin said, scribbling in his notepad. "We got a location out of him. He said he was backstage."

"Okay?" I said sarcastically. "That doesn't mean anything."

"It's just another thing to check out, ain't it?" Gavin said. "If we're investigating this, then we should investigate *all* of it, right?"

"Right," I said reluctantly. It wasn't that I didn't want to find the kid with the hockey mask – it was that I didn't want to waste time checking out a lead that didn't matter.

"Meet me in the morning before school?" Gavin asked. "We'll check out the backstage area during homeroom and see if we can't find anything back there."

I nodded. "Until then," I sighed.

Gavin must not have heard the sarcasm in my voice, or if he did then he didn't care. He patted me on the shoulder and walked back to the exit of the library while I remained in place.

Eli ended up having nothing to do with the talent show disaster, that much was obvious, but I had to remind myself that at least we were getting a direction. Who knows, maybe Gavin was right, and there was something worth investigating backstage. If anything, all this work was a nice distraction from whatever Wyatt was up to, and for me, a distraction like that was worth a thousand bucks.

Sophia and Eli had both mentioned someone named Calvin. Gavin and I have both never heard of the kid. Whoever he was, he was beginning to look like someone that we *needed* to question because from what Sophia and Eli had said, he was there when Hotcakes was set free.

Wednesday. 7:45 AM. The cafeteria.

The bell rang just as I stepped into the cafeteria. It was Wednesday so there were still two days left to set up for the talent show. Zoe had convinced Principal Davis to host the talent show during the first half of the school day on Friday so everyone would have to miss their morning classes. Nobody complained about it because it was an awesome idea. I suspect even the teachers thought it would be a nice break from the normal routine of handling a roomful of loud students.

"Over here, Chase," Gavin said, standing next to my cousin and Faith.

Zoe looked up at me and smiled. When I approached her, she put her arms around me and gave me a hug.

"What's that for?" I asked.

"It's because I hate being mad at you," Zoe said. "I'm still *not* happy with you, but at least I'm not mad anymore."

"It's a start," I said, smiling.

"Have you guys heard of someone named Calvin?" Gavin asked, pulling his notepad from his pocket and flipping it open.

Zoe crinkled her nose. "Hmmm," she hummed. "That kid who stole the time capsule that one time?"

"No, that's Brody," Faith said. "And I think he was cleared of those charges – something about being framed and whatnot."

"She's right," I said. "That's Brody Valentine. I actually know him. I don't think he'd do anything as vicious as breaking a stage or anything like that."

"That's right," Zoe said, nodding. "Then I don't know anyone named Calvin."

"Sophia and Eli *both* said they saw Calvin messing around with the cage before Hotcakes got free," Gavin said.

Faith snorted, and then covered her mouth instantly. "Hotcakes is the name of the penguin? I *like* it."

Gavin ignored her comment. He turned to my cousin and spoke. "Did you see anyone by the penguin's cage that morning?"

Zoe hummed, thinking as her eyes glazed over. "I couldn't tell you," she said. "I was so distracted by a bunch of other stuff that morning."

Faith jumped up and sat on the tabletop next to us, resting her arms on her knees. "You think Calvin might be the kid in the hockey mask?"

I raised my eyebrows. "Maybe. We just don't know for sure yet."

"No leads except for someone named Calvin, huh?" Faith asked.

"Not a single one," I replied. "On the bright side, we know that Olive and Wyatt are dating now."

"*No way!*" Faith said. "That's a recipe for disaster if I've ever heard one! That's as bad as squeezing a lemon into your eyes after cutting onions!"

"It's as bad as getting a paper cut on your eyeball!" Gavin said, cringing at his own joke.

Zoe chimed in. "It's as bad as a ninja who punched themself in the face because they thought they were quick enough to dodge their own attack."

Gavin laughed. "It's as bad as a ninja who forgot their uniform at home so they had to borrow their mom's leggings!"

"Oh good," I said sarcastically. "We're making fun of me again."

All three of my friends LOL'd.

A huge smile was beaming across Zoe's face, which made me happy. "We make fun of you 'cause you're our friend," she said. "Come on, lighten up. We all do it to each other."

I smiled, knowing she was right. Then I tried to make a joke myself. "It's as bad as tipping a cow over while it sleeps!"

My friends gasped, horrified.

"Whoa, major burn on cows, dude!" Gavin said, upset.

Zoe jumped up from the table, angry. "Yeah, man. Why would anyone ever do that to a cow? Are you some kind of monster or something?"

"What'd a cow ever do to you?" Faith asked, disappointed.

"Serious?" I asked, watching Zoe and Faith walk away. "It was a joke! I heard people used to do that for fun! I would never do that to a cow! I *love* cows!"

Gavin jumped up from the table. "Can't win 'em all," he said.

"Whatever," I said. "Let's just get back stage and see if we can find anything that might help us figure out who the kid in the hockey mask was."

Several minutes later, Gavin and I were digging around the backstage of the cafeteria. It was spooky how often I'd seen the area since I started school at Buchanan. It was almost like evil grew from somewhere back there.

Gavin scanned the floor, searching for anything that would be useful. I pushed my hands in my pockets as I hobbled down the narrow passage. There was so much junk and boxes filled with random things that it was almost impossible to walk freely.

I stepped over a thick braided rope, recognizing it from a

few days ago. It was the same rope that had been tied to the scaffolding in the cafeteria. The only reason I remembered it was because it had hot pink and green threads running through the braids. I followed the rope again with my eyes, seeing that it ran down the narrow corridor and out into the cafeteria. Apparently it was still attached to the scaffolding.

"We're never gonna find anything back here," I said, pushing the rope aside with my foot.

"You don't know that," Gavin replied. "The worst thing you can do is *not* help."

"I'm helping!" I said defensively. "Who said I wasn't helping?"

"You're standin' around pouting!" Gavin said. "Make yourself useful and look for something, *anything*, that doesn't belong!"

"This place is filled with random junk!" I said. "*Nothing* belongs back here!"

"Then look for something that sticks out more than normal," Gavin said, but stopped instantly. "Did you hear that?"

I stopped in my tracks. "Hear what?"

The faint sound of tapping answered my question. *Clickety clickety clickety.*

"What *was* that?" I asked.

Gavin shrugged his shoulders. "Iunno," he grunted, too lazy to actually form the words, "I don't know."

Clickety clickety clickety.

"There it is again!" Gavin said.

Clickety clickety clickety.

"It's getting closer," I whispered, afraid.

Clickety clickety clickety clickety clickety clickety.

I stumbled backward, hearing the tapping sounds get closer and closer. The clicks were maddening and loud inside my head. It sounded like a monster tapping its claws on the floor.

And then came the squawk sound that made me snap.

Squaaaaaaaaaawk!

I didn't stop to see what it was. I turned around and tried to run down the hall, but stumbled over the boxes behind me. Several props from the drama club spilled to the floor, including all kinds of hockey masks. There must've been a dozen of them laying on the floor beside me.

I slid the masks around with my feet. The kid Gavin and I chased after must've gotten his mask from this box, which would make perfect sense since the scooters were stolen from the drama club too.

I looked back to see if Gavin noticed the masks, but I saw that he was already sprinting away in the other direction.

Squaaaaaaaaaawk!

My heart skipped a beat, remembering that a monster was after me. Pushing the hockey masks away from me, I rolled back to my feet and moved down the narrow passage. The tapping sounds were getting louder and sounded as if they were right behind me.

There was no way I was going to look back. I was too scared that I'd be frozen in fear at the sight of whatever it was that was chasing after me.

The passage grew darker as I ran farther into it. The walls began to pinch together making me slow my escape and walk sideways. The tapping sound grew louder and faster as I moved

slower and slower. It was like a terrible nightmare. Finally, I made it to the end of the corridor. A short stack of cardboard boxes stood before me, basically telling me I couldn't go any further.
Clenching my jaw, I turned slowly to see my attacker.

The space in front of me was empty. The silence was now scarier than the tapping I had heard only seconds ago. I shut my eyes and took a deep breath, trying my hardest not to pass out from fear.

When I opened my eyes again, I stared into space, allowing myself to see everything by focusing on nothing. It's a ninja technique where you stare into space and allow your peripheral vision to do what it does best, which is to see movement off to the side that you're not looking at.

I stared into the open space in front of me, breathing slowly. The corridor was completely still, as I took a step out.

And then a small black creature twitched in the shadows. I flinched, feeling my heart drop until I realized what it was I was looking at.

Not even ten feet away stood the missing penguin, staring at me with its head cocked sideways. If it could talk, it would've been like, "Dude, what's *wrong* with you?"

Needless to say, I felt a little dumb for not realizing it was the penguin chasing me, but in my defense, I was in a dark hallway and thought I was going to die.

Hotcakes hopped forward once, and dropped something from his beak. A folded slip of paper gently landed on the floor. And then the black and white animal squawked once more before disappearing into an open air vent nearby.

I slid out from the spot I was hiding in. "Someone should really fix all these open vents," I whispered as I picked up the slip of paper. It was wet from the penguin's beak. When I unfolded it, I couldn't believe my eyes. It was a note addressed to the letter "A."

A,
The penguin plan didn't work out, but we have one more shot on Friday morning. I won't mess it up this time.

There wasn't a signature.
I studied the note for a moment. It *had* to be the talent show

71

it was referring to because it mentioned the penguin, but it was obvious that there was *more* going on than anyone suspected. It sounded like the penguin was only *part* of the equation. Could it have been a distraction so someone could try to wreck the stage?

"I won't mess it up this time," I whispered, reading the note out loud.

Mess up what? Was it possible that they wanted to break more than just a corner of the stage? My stomach felt sick.

Looking at the open air vent, I tightened my lips at the thought of the black and white bird that dropped the note off. Was it on purpose? Was it trying to solve this mystery too? Could Brayden have been right? Are penguins smarter than everyone thought?

So many questions!

I heard footsteps close in on my position. When I looked up from the note, I saw Gavin in the narrow passage.

"You okay?" he asked, but before I could answer, he said, "It was the penguin, wasn't it? I realized it as soon as I jumped back into the cafeteria."

I laughed. "I realized the same thing as soon as I saw I couldn't run anymore."

"Did he freak out at you?"

I shook my head, handing my friend the note. "Nope, but it left me this."

Taking the wet note in his hands, Gavin read it silently. "It's addressed to someone who goes by 'A,'" he said. "That penguin left this for you?"

"I know, right? Weird," I said, walking back to the cafeteria. "Maybe Zoe will know who the note's referring to."

A few minutes later Gavin and I were sitting at a table back in the cafeteria. The room was completely empty since everyone had left for their first period class.

Zoe held the note in her hands, chewing on her lip the way she did when she was concentrating. "A..." she whispered. Her eyes looked past the note and at me. "You found this back there?"

I scratched the back of my neck. "Uh, yeah. I *found* it. We'll go with that."

"Why's it wet?" Zoe asked, rotating the note in her hands.

I set my hands on the table and sighed. "The penguin gave it to me."

Immediately, Zoe dropped the note on the table. "*Ew! Serious?* That was in the penguin's *mouth?*"

Gavin laughed. "A little bit of penguin spit ain't gonna hurt ya."

Zoe cocked an eyebrow. "Um, have you heard of a little thing called bacteria? Actually, *millions* of little things that make up bacteria?" She stretched her fingers out in front of her as if she didn't want to risk touching anything. "So gross, you guys. Seriously, *sick.*"

I put my hand over the note and slid it back to me. "Do you know anyone who goes by the letter A?"

Zoe pulled out a sanitary wipe from her book bag and tore open the package. I wasn't surprised to see that she carried something like that with her. Scrubbing her fingers with the wipe, she spoke. "I don't know anyone who just goes by A, no. But I *do* know an *Adam* that works for me. He's one of the guys backstage. He helps guide kids through the back before and after their act.

Adam's also in charge of making sure the curtain goes up and down when it needs to."

Gavin sighed like an old cowboy as he stood from the table. "Looks like this whole mess is *messier* than we thought."

"It seems there's more going on here than just a penguin getting set free," I said. "It's beginning to look like it wasn't just a childish prank."

Zoe frowned and started chewing her lip again. "All I wanted to do was put on a talent show. I wanted to bring some fun to the school, and some jerk has to go and try to ruin things."

I remained silent. Gavin didn't say anything either. He just reached across the table and set his hand on my cousin's hand. It must've helped because she smiled softly at him. Gross.

The three of us decided to meet back at the cafeteria before lunch. Adam was next on the list to question, even though we weren't a hundred percent certain the note was addressed to him.

As I walked away from Gavin and my cousin, I felt a chill travel down my spine, just as I had when walking into school Monday morning. Bad things were happening at Buchanan, and my friends and I were smack-dab in the middle of all of it.

Wednesday. 10:45 AM. Gym class.

I was the last one out of the gymnasium and the only one wearing a goofy looking moose mascot. The inside of the head was beginning to smell a little funky from not being washed properly. Why couldn't I have picked a cooler mascot than a moose? Why not a knight? Or a Viking? Man, why didn't I choose a super huge robot instead? Total missed opportunity on my part.

Jake pointed his finger and said some pretty insulting stuff as I took my place on the sidelines. I tried to play it off by clutching my belly and moving my shoulders up and down like I was laughing.

"Hey, coach!" Jake shouted. "We want that dumb moose on our team! Can we do that?"

Coach Cooper waved his hand with a huge grin from the gym doors. He obviously couldn't hear a word Jake was saying.

Jake pointed at me. "If you feel like scoring another touchdown for us today, feel free to, alright?"

Like a goon, I set one of my hands on my hips and wagged my finger at him like I was disagreeing. I felt like such a nimrod.

Pacing back and forth next to the field, I watched as Brayden's team got owned by Jake's. Every time Jake's team scored a touchdown, I made the mascot look like he was disappointed. Every time Brayden's team scored, I decided I'd jump up and down, doing a happy dance – too bad Brayden's team *never* scored.

As I watched the game go on, I listened to the sound of my

own breathing inside the mask. Since I wasn't doing anything and had nobody to talk to, I thought about the kid in the hockey mask. I took advantage of the fact that I had the whole period to sit and think inside the moose costume.

The penguin was set free before school on Monday, which was during the time that Zoe and our friends began setting things up for the talent show. The penguin was part of an act in the show and was there on Monday morning because Zoe wanted all the acts to run through a rehearsal five days before the actual show.

While the penguin was set free, someone broke one of the corners of the stage that Gavin was building. Then the kid took off with a scooter taken from the drama club, which was the moment that I showed up. The kid was wearing a hockey mask, which turned out to be just another prop from the drama club taken from one of their boxes backstage.

At that moment, I felt something bump against me, but I ignored it so I wouldn't lose my train of thought.

Sophia was the name Zoe gave us to speak to first, but she turned out to be a dead-end. And then Sophia namedropped Eli, but the only thing he was good for was telling us that he was working with the paint cans backstage.

Both Sophia and Eli mentioned someone named Calvin, who we have yet to speak with. Gavin and I have never heard of the kid so we're still in the process of figuring out who exactly he is.

After that, the penguin dropped the note from its little beak – the note that was addressed to the letter "A." Zoe then told us someone named Adam works backstage for the talent show. I guess he's next on the list for us to question.

That's basically everything up to this point.

I blinked, returning back to gym class, surprised to see everyone staring at me. Members of Jake's wolf pack were running at full speed in my direction. It was just like the day before except I wasn't holding...

When I looked down, I saw the football in my hands. I must've caught it when I was zoned out! That was probably the bump I ignored a few seconds before then.

My ninja skills kicked in again, and without warning. If I had thought about it, I probably would've just dropped the ball because I had no desire to make a fool of myself again, but my legs were already running.

Jake's teammates dove at me again. The first few were easy to dodge. All I had to do was dig my foot into the grass to switch directions and they sailed right past me.

Three other kids stood between the end zone and me. I made sure to take a mental note about where the sun was just in case I got mixed up again. It was shining directly in front of me as I ran toward Jake and his team. All I had to do was keep running for the sun and I'd be fine.

The first kid threw her arms out, trying to tackle me. I arched my back and sped up as my moose helmet bobbed on my shoulders. I felt her fingers scrape against my side, but she was unable to grab ahold of my shirt. I heard her grunt as she landed on the ground.

The second kid dipped his head down and barreled toward me like a train, which if you had any ninja training, you'd know that was the worst mistake an enemy could make. He was committing himself to a move that either had a success or failure option! All I had to do was step slightly to the side as he ran by, rolling against his train motion. And that's exactly what I did. I spun in a circle against him, which made him plow into the field.

But I didn't stop moving. There was one last kid standing in the way of a touchdown. It was Jake, the leader of the wolf pack, and apparently a member of Wyatt's red ninja clan.

I clenched my teeth and ran at full speed toward the end zone. Jake sprinted for me as I curved around him. I glanced at the sun one last time to make sure it was still in front of me. The blinding light reassured me that I was okay.

With huge strides, I ran into the end zone, scoring the only touchdown Brayden's team had scored all week. An eruption of applause came from far behind me as I turned around, lifting both hands in victory.

Suddenly, Jake slammed into me, tackling me to the ground. The grass and dirt burned my elbows as I slid against earth. My head bounced like a golf ball inside the moose helmet. Finally, my body stopped, laying out in the open grass, and in the worst searing pain imaginable.

I continued to squint at the sun through the eyes of the

mask, but a shadow loomed over me, blocking out the light. It was Jake, staring at me through the eyes of the mask.

"So that's where you've been all week," Jake whispered.

I tried to say something smart, but it only came out as a painful groan.

Coach Cooper's bear horn went off again just at that instant, signaling the end of gym.

Jake glanced away, and then back to me. "This isn't over, Chase. You embarrassed me out here today, and you'll get what's coming to you. Tomorrow. *Tomorrow.*"

Jake picked himself off the ground and jogged back to the locker rooms. Brayden helped me to my feet. I brushed the grass off my scraped up body and took the mask off my head. The cold air felt good against my smashed up face. Brayden and I made our way back to the locker rooms, joking about how much we hated gym class.

Jake had pummeled me *after* I scored a touchdown, but to be fair, I shouldn't have been in the game to begin with. I was only supposed to be the mascot!

Wednesday. 11:40 AM. Lunch.

It took me a little longer than normal to get cleaned up in the locker room. Coach Cooper joked about me getting tackled in gym mostly because the mascot usually doesn't get on the field. He was cool about it though – he asked if it was because someone was being a jerk on the field, but I told him no since I don't blame Jake for tackling me. I was asking for it by trying to score the touchdown in my moose mask.

The second I stepped out of the gym, Sophia cornered me. She was hugging her textbooks close to her body. "Chase! Have you found Hotcakes yet?"

I shook my head sadly. "No, not yet, but we're still trying."

Sophia frowned. "It's been *two* days. Hotcakes has been on his own for *two* days!"

I could see the tears forming in her eyes. I wasn't sure what to say. "Uh, yeah. It's cool though. I'm sure he's fine."

Shaking her head, Sophia spoke softly. "He's on his own and probably starving. I feel terrible for letting him out of my sight for even a second! It wasn't supposed to be like that!"

"No," I said, shaking my head. "You're right. We should've found him right after he escaped. I'm sorry that we haven't yet."

Sophia looked up at me. Her eyes sparkled from the tears that were swelling in them. Biting her lower lip, she turned around and sped off. If this were a television show, I'd probably go after her, but since this was real life, I had no idea what to do.

She looked *so* sad that my heart broke.

79

After a few minutes, I met Gavin outside the cafeteria. He was standing with Zoe and Faith who were cupping their hands on the tinted windows.

"Is he in there?" I asked as I approached my friends.

Zoe didn't move from her spot. Her breath was fogging up the glass in front of her face. "Yeah, he's sitting with a bunch of his friends."

Faith didn't look up from the glass either. "He's kinda cute, isn't he?"

I'm not sure why exactly, but Faith's comment upset me a little. I cupped my hands on the glass and squinted through the window. Adam was toward the back of the room. He was dressed like a prepster, wearing a buttoned up shirt, tan khaki pants, and brown loafers. His brown hair was slicked back, styled like one of those 1960s actors. "Whatever, he's not *that* good looking."

Faith laughed. "Jealous much?"

"Whatever," I said, stepping away from the window. I pushed the door to the lunchroom wide open and marched inside.

Gavin hustled to keep up with me. "Easy, tiger," he said jokingly. "I'm sure Faith didn't mean anything by that."

I stopped in the middle of the aisle, standing in the way of a bunch of kids, making them walk around us. "Just tell me what the plan is," I said, unsure exactly about why I was unhappy.

Gavin took a breath as he scratched at his chin, carefully considering our options.

Adam was at one of the tables on the east side of the cafeteria, closest to the stage. The group of students he was sitting with were members of the drama club. I recognized a few of the kids from one of the plays they had performed recently. Adam wasn't in the play, but even stagehands were considered part of the club.

The lunchroom felt empty just like the day before. It was weird to see half filled tables as students were sprinkled across the cafeteria. Was there some sort of weeklong field trip I wasn't aware of? Where'd everyone go?

Gavin took the lead as usual and approached the table. "Play along, alright?"

"What's the plan, boss?" I asked.

"Good cop, bad cop," Gavin replied.

"What's that?"

Gavin glanced over his shoulder at me. "One of us acts really nice to the kid," he explained. "And then one of us acts like a jerk to him. It'll make it easier for Adam to talk to the good cop, hopefully spilling everything he knows about what happened on Monday. So when we get up here, I'll go first, okay?"

I nodded. Perfect. Gavin was going to be the cool nice guy while I had to figure out how to act bad. I'm not a mean kid at heart, but for some reason I actually *felt* angry with Adam. I don't know why because I've never talked to the kid in my life! And don't say it was because Faith said he was cute. I was already over that... I think.

As we approached the table, I overheard Adam talking. "So yeah, that bike's gonna cost three hundred bucks so I'll definitely get it. That'll leave me with a little extra for comic books."

Gavin stopped at Adam's table and waited patiently for them to notice. When they did, he slapped the table with his open palm. The crack echoed across the noisy cafeteria, silencing half the students in the room. *"Where were you on Monday morning?"* he shouted, pointing at Adam's face.

ADAM

Adam flinched, scooting his chair away from the table. His friends looked at each other, confused about the angry kid standing at their table. "What the—*What's your deal, man?*" Adam growled.

"*Where were you?*" Gavin shouted again.

I stood silently behind Gavin, balling my fists, nervously waiting my turn.

Slapping the table again, Gavin spoke through his clenched teeth. "*Monday morning! You'd better tell me before—*"

I took that as my cue. Stepping in front of Gavin, I raised my hands and made them look like claws. Darting my eyes back and forth, I growled like a dinosaur as I tried to talk, but since I wasn't sure what to say, I just said, "*I'm crazy!*"

Everyone at the table giggled at my dinosaur impression.

Gavin stepped backward and looked at me, puzzled. "Dude, *what* are you doing?"

I torqued my head the way I thought a dinosaur would. "I'm doing the bad cop thing," I hissed.

"No, *I'm* the bad cop," Gavin snipped. "You're the *good* cop!"

"We can't both be the *bad* cops!" I said. "Can we?"

Adam sat forward and laughed heartily. "You guys are trying to do the good cop, bad cop thing? Looks more like the bad *actor* cop, *pterodactyl* cop thing."

Instantly, I dropped my arms down to my side and stood straight. I know it was an insult, but I hardly noticed since I was thinking of how awesome a pterodactyl cop would be.

Gavin sighed. "Look, man. We just want to know where you were on Monday morning?"

"In here," Adam said, looking at the rest of the cafeteria.

"What are you doing for the talent show?" Gavin asked.

"Nothing," Adam replied. "I'm just one of the stagehands. I'm backstage the entire time."

"What do you know about Hotcakes?" I asked.

Adam shrugged his shoulder. "I like 'em? Pancakes are my favorite thing for breakfast."

"Hotcakes, the *penguin*," I said, irked.

"Oh, *that*," Adam replied nervously. He tapped at the table with his fingers. "No clue."

I took the note the penguin had dropped and set it on the table in front of him.

Adam's face remained unchanged as if he were a statue. "Where'd you find that?"

"A friend gave it to me," I said, smiling. "You recognize it, don't you?"

Adam paused. His chest rose slowly as he took a breath. At last, he spoke. "Whatever. You guys are pullin' my chain, aren't you? I wasn't anywhere *near* that penguin on Monday. Is that what you need to hear? I was backstage the entire time! I had nothing to do with the penguin, or the busted stage, or that kid that burst into the hallway with a hockey mask and scooter."

"He got the mask and scooter from the drama club boxes backstage," I said. "Did you see anyone poking around back there before Hotcakes was set free?"

Adam smirked. "I saw a lot of kids poking around backstage

before that penguin got loose. It was rehearsal so everyone was busy doing something."

Adam had a point. There would've been tons of activity all over the cafeteria on Monday morning. Everyone helping with the talent show was probably busy with something so anyone could've easily set Hotcakes free without any witnesses.

Sighing, I shut my eyes and pinched the bridge of my nose the same way my dad did when trying to relieve a headache. When I looked at Gavin, I could tell he was frustrated too.

So far the entire investigation had been nothing but dead-end after dead-end. The talent show was only two days away, and we were basically still at the starting line as far as figuring out *who* the kid in the hockey mask was.

The only real lead we had was a note addressed to someone named "A." With as many "A" names as there were at Buchanan, the odds were against us that we even had the right one. It could've even been a girl!

Adam paused and then pointed at me. "You know who you need to ask? That Calvin kid. I'm pretty sure he was jostling that bird's cage on Monday. I remember because I *scolded* him for doing it." Adam lifted his finger and tapped it toward us as if he were pushing an imaginary button. "And y'know what? Now that I think of it, I saw him messing with the drama club's stuff back there too! Yeah, I remember him playing with a hockey mask!"

That was it! Finally, a connection that *meant* something. If Adam had seen Calvin take the hockey mask from the back room, then that might've been enough to lead to the full truth. The only problem was that we still didn't know who Calvin was. My stomach turned, realizing that this new kid was definitely going to be a problem for us. He was going to be another bully in the sea of bullies at Buchanan School.

Gavin made eye contact with me, and then looked back at Adam. "*Who's* Calvin? Is he in the cafeteria right now?"

Again, Adam paused, blinking rapidly as he turned his vision toward the students in the room. "Calvin? He's a kid about medium height, sorta gangly. Um… he's got short brown hair, brown eyes, and wears a lot of t-shirt and jeans outfits."

I rubbed my eyebrows, feeling a tiny headache coming on. "So he looks like every kid at this school," I said.

Shrugging his shoulders, Adam tightened a smile. "What can I tell ya? He looks like you. Oh, he's also a new kid here. Maybe that's why you haven't heard of him yet."

I folded my arms, scanning the room for anyone who looked like the person Adam had described. Yep, he was right. A lot of the students looked about the same height and body shape. This wasn't going to be easy.

"Actually, I think he had a white patch of hair on his head," Adam added. "Yeah, now that I think of it, I remember seeing that and thinking it was weird."

"Some kids have that kind of birthmark," Gavin said, writing in his notepad. When he was finished, he flipped it shut. Just as he had done before, Gavin smiled gently, and said, "Thank you for your time."

Adam tilted his head like he was wearing a hat to bid us farewell. "Not a problem."

The bell rang as Gavin and I walked away from Adam and his friends. All the students in the cafeteria stood from their tables to walk their trash to the garbage cans along the walls. Zoe and Faith were waiting for us at the lunchroom doors.

"What'd you find out?" Zoe asked. "Was he the one that did it?"

Gavin shook his head. "No, but we might've gotten a solid lead."

"Calvin's name was mentioned *again*," I said. "But this time there was more. Adam said he saw Calvin messing around with the hockey masks backstage!"

Zoe clenched her fist. "Got him!"

"So where is he?" Faith asked. "What's he look like?"

Gavin pointed his thumb at me and laughed. "Like *him*."

"Har har," I said, faking a laugh. "Calvin is supposedly the same height and weight as me. Brown hair, brown eyes, y'know, all that super handsome stuff."

That time, Zoe faked the laugh. "Har har."

"He's got a birthmark in his hair though," I continued. "Adam said he saw a white patch on the back of Calvin's head, so all we gotta do is find someone with a patch of white hair!"

"Great," Faith sighed. "In a school filled with a thousand students, finding one will be a piece of cake."

Zoe giggled. She looked at me and spoke. "What if this was like one of your weird science fiction movies? And *you* were Calvin, but you didn't know it!"

Faith's eyes grew wide as she danced her fingers in the air. "Ooooooooooooooo!" she sang.

I couldn't help but laugh.

Gavin clapped his hands together. "Alright then," he said joyfully. "We'll all meet here again before lunch tomorrow and search for this kid. I have a feeling we're getting closer to the truth, which is a good thing."

Zoe and Gavin stepped out of the lunchroom, holding hands *again*. Faith jogged down the hall ahead of me so she could get to her locker and make it on time to science before the bell rang.

I stood in the lobby, staring at the spot on the carpet where the kid in the hockey mask knocked me over. My vision blurred as I thought about all the problems I was having to deal with that week, which to a sixth grader, was *a lot.*

I hadn't forgotten about the fact that Wyatt had stolen the room my ninja clan trained in. It was a bold move on his part, but an unsurprising one too. He'd do anything to flip my life upside down, and he was getting really good at it. Hopefully once this whole ordeal with the talent show was over with, I could try to get to the bottom of whatever evil scheme he was up to.

First, Wyatt teams up with President Sebastian. Second, he starts going out with Olivia Jones! There *should* be red flags raising everywhere in the school, but unfortunately, nobody seemed to care! But I could feel it in my bones – there was *something* going on behind the scenes at Buchanan School. I just didn't know what it was.

My eyes followed the black skid marks on the carpet as they curved and disappeared down the hallway. Goosebumps rose on my neck as I stared at the black stripe burnt into the carpet. Calvin was a new student at Buchanan, but had already caused enough trouble to disrupt an entire talent show.

We only had one full day of school until the talent show on Friday morning. Hopefully, Gavin and I would find Calvin right away the next day. That would be ideal, but with my luck, we probably wouldn't find him at all.

Thursday. 7:45 AM. The cafeteria.

The next morning, I entered the cafeteria expecting to see the same thing I had for the past few days so I was surprised when I didn't.

Stepping through the door, I had to weave my way through the crowd of students that had gathered in the room. I couldn't see Zoe anywhere, or *any* of my friends for that matter. I gripped my book bag straps, kept my head down, and pushed my way forward.

From where I was standing, I couldn't see the stage, but I could see the kids who were *standing* on the stage. Gavin must have completed the repairs before I got to school.

Red, blue, and yellow lights danced circles on the walls, flickering on and off. Someone was also messing with the strobe light at the back of the room, giving me a tiny migraine as the bright light blinked rapidly.

The speaker system had been hooked up too. A loud squeal came from the huge black boxes at the front of the room. Everyone cupped their hands over their ears, shielding themselves from the ear piercing tone.

The speakers thumped twice before Zoe's voice cut through them. "Check, check, one, two, checkinnnnnnng, checkinnnnnng. Can you guys hear me? Am I coming through okay?"

Most of the students nodded "yes" in response.

"Awesome. Let's get started shall we?" she said, jumping onto the stage. I watched as she took command of the room. Grabbing one of the microphones, she spoke. "First off, I'd like to thank everyone for being here this morning and for participating in this rehearsal. You all know it was supposed to be last Monday, but was rudely interrupted by some hijinks." Zoe turned toward Sophia who was standing backstage. "We haven't found Hotcakes yet, but we will."

Sophia dabbed at her red nose with a ball of tissue and nodded.

Zoe went on. "We're going to go through everyone's acts this morning exactly the same way we'll do it tomorrow. That way we all know what to expect."

I made my way to the front of the room until I was next to the stage. Gavin and Faith were off to the side, watching my cousin wrap up her announcements.

Zoe pointed at the long bench at the side of the room, under the scaffolding with the paint cans. "So the first thing I'm going to have everyone do is sit over there on the bench next to the wall. You're going to sit in the order of when your act will perform, so the first act will take the first spot, the second act will take the second, and so on…"

Everyone in the room shuffled their feet and started moving toward the long bench on the wall. The scaffolding with the paint cans was still directly above the bench, which was weird, but since it was just a rehearsal, I figured it would be gone by the next day.

"Howdy," Gavin said like a cowboy.

"S'up?" I said. "Any sign of Calvin?"

"Nope," Gavin said. He pointed to the side of the room, where many of the students had already taken a seat, waiting their turn for rehearsal. "He'll probably be over there somewhere though."

Sophia jumped in front of us out of nowhere. "Anything yet?" she asked, hopeful.

Gavin shook his head and stared at the floor.

"Not yet," I said. "But we know Hotcakes is alright. I've seen him a couple times this week, but wasn't able to catch him."

Sophia's eyes lit up as she cupped her hand over her mouth. "Oh! That's good! So he's okay?"

"As far as I can tell, yeah," I replied loudly so she could hear me over the noise in the lunchroom.

Sophia grabbed my arm. "If you see him, you just have to

88

yell his name! He responds to that! It's a game he likes to play! I promise he's a good penguin! He won't bite you or anything! My family has raised him since he was a little baby!"

I nodded. "So just yell *'Hotcakes'* as loudly as I can?"

"Yes!" she said. "I promise you that he'll stop in place and let you to pick him up! He won't bite! I swear!"

I glanced at Gavin, but he wasn't paying attention to Sophia. He was too busy examining the room for a kid with a patch of white hair.

When I turned back to Sophia, she was gone without a trace... until I turned to my left and saw that she had returned to her spot on the bench. Coincidentally she was seated next to Eli. They must have been the first two acts in the show because they were right up front. The bench stretched out behind them, filled with the rest of the students who were also waiting their turn. It was a little strange how they were seated because they were the only two students who *weren't* under the scaffolding.

The metal scaffolding was still above the bench. I only noticed it because it was unlike Zoe to leave something like that unfinished. It was possible that she just didn't have enough people to help her get it out of the way. No big deal, I thought. I could probably get Gavin and Brayden to help me slide it backstage later.

I turned to Gavin, but before I could say anything, everyone on the bench screamed, flinching backward at the same time. Some of the students scrambled to the floor and started running to the back of the cafeteria. I looked at Gavin who was just as confused as I was. The lunchroom was suddenly a mess of confusing shouts.

"It's over there! Behind the stage!"

"It looks angry! Somebody catch that thing!"

"The penguin! Someone grab that penguin! It's at the back of the room!"

I spun in place, looking at the spot everyone was screaming about. They were right. The penguin was hopping back and forth, flapping its itty bitty wings as it danced.

"Get it!" Zoe shouted into the microphone from the stage.

Immediately, I dashed forward. The penguin was all the way across the room so I sprinted as hard as I could. I heard the sound of tribal drums booming in my head as my feet hit the floor, and then I realized that someone was testing the sound system with

89

their music.

The penguin bolted when it saw me running at it. Like I said before, those little birds move way faster than you'd expect. The black and white animal ran along the wall until it made it to the stage. It hopped up and raced across the wooden floor.

I kept my eye on it as it disappeared backstage again. It must've been living back there for the first half of the week.

The science teacher, Mrs. Olsen, lifted herself onto the stage and walked carefully just in case the bird jumped out. She was hunched over, staring daggers at the spot where the penguin had disappeared.

I stopped just behind Mrs. Olsen and remembered what Sophia had said. Taking a deep breath, I leaned forward and shouted, "*Wait up, Hotcakes!*"

Mrs. Olsen spun around and glared at me. "*Excuse* me, young man? How *dare* you say such an inappropriate thing to me!"

A roar of laughter erupted from all the students behind me.

I didn't stop to explain myself to the science teacher. Running to the side of the stage, I climbed the stairs and made my way backstage, feeling the blood pump through my veins.

Gavin dodged Mrs. Olsen and slid across the polished surface of the stage until bouncing to his feet. "We're getting this bird today!" he shouted as he ran past me.

When I caught up with Gavin, he was standing just beyond the stage curtain, out of view from everyone in the cafeteria. The pitter patter of tiny penguin feet drifted in the air. "Where'd he go?" I asked.

Gavin was catching his breath. "I saw him slip into that vent," he said, pointing at the air vent behind a cardboard box. The opening was about three feet high by three feet wide, as large as a small door. He slid the box out of the way and knelt down, staring into the metal passageway.

"I don't know about this," I said, looking at the vent.

"No, look," Gavin said as he reached into the opening. He pushed his hand against the back wall. It fell over with a metal clang. "This just goes through the wall. It's not an air vent at all. It's... *fake*."

"What?" I asked, confused. I got down to my knees and saw what my friend was talking about. The air vent wasn't actually an air vent. It looked more like a hidden door or something.

"Come on," Gavin said, crawling through the passage. "I saw the penguin go through here."

I nodded, questioning my ability to make smart decisions rather than dangerous and irresponsible ones. "Alright, but let's just get that bird and get out of here. I don't like the looks of this."

On the other side, Gavin and I stood to our feet. The ceiling was low enough that we had to crouch a bit in order to walk. The short hallway we were in was dark and colder than the rest of the school. It smelled musty and felt damp.

I looked at the floor expecting to see a dirt path, but was surprised to see that the ground we were walking on was tiled, which meant that at some point in time, this narrow hallway was probably used quite frequently.

"You hear that?" Gavin asked.

I stopped, listening carefully until I heard it. I swallowed hard as I listened to the sound of a thousand thumps at the same time. Slapping noises bounced off the walls and into my ears as I started to walk forward silently. Muffled voices shouted at each other, but they weren't saying anything in particular. Just, "Hi-ya!" Holding my breath, I stared down the hall, knowing exactly what the sound was.

There were ninjas nearby, and they were training.

"We should turn back," Gavin said, suddenly realizing the same thing I did.

I lifted my hand, gesturing for my friend to keep quiet. "No way," I said. "This is *huge*. This *has* to be where Wyatt and the red ninjas have been training!"

"So that's fine," Gavin whispered nervously. "You can explore this area *later* when they're *not* here!"

"I can't leave," I said. Ever since my ninja outfit was stolen a few months back, I had been wearing my new ninja outfit under my street clothes. And in that passageway, I was extremely happy I had it with me. Pulling my ninja mask over my face, I spoke through the fabric. "I have to see this for myself. I need to know how large his clan has grown. Just be cool and follow my lead."

"Be cool? That's easy for you to say!" Gavin whispered harshly. "You're wearing a mask! Where's *my* mask? A ninja mask would be pretty helpful for me right about now!"

I ignored Gavin's whining and continued to walk forward, listening as the thumping sounds of ninjas grew louder. After a few twists and turns, I found myself at the end of the passage, where there was another square opening in the wall.

Finally, I made it close enough that I could peek my head out a little. What I saw was the most frightening thing I had ever seen in my life. The red ninjas were training, just as I had suspected, but their numbers were larger than I ever imagined.

The room opened up just beyond the entrance in the wall. It looked like an abandoned greenhouse or something because the ceiling was made out of glass that was caked with dirt. The sun was shining outside, but the room was dark. Book bags were set on tables against one of the walls; tables that looked like they had been used to carry plants.

Taped up to the wall next to us was a motivational poster that had a silhouette of a ninja and training times. From the text, I could see that the red ninjas trained before school and *during* lunch.

I smiled.

Of course! That explained why *half* the students were missing from the cafeteria! And then my smile disappeared once I realized it also meant *half* the sixth graders were members of the red ninja clan. Wyatt was creating an army.

"Whoa," Gavin whispered by my side. "This is bad."

"Ya think?" I said.

"Is Hotcakes in there?"

I scanned the room. "No, I don't see him."

"Wait a sec," Gavin said, pushing me aside. "Am I crazy, or is that President Sebastian?"

I looked at the front of the room. As much as I wished it were true, Gavin *wasn't* crazy. President Sebastian was talking to Wyatt as they watched the red ninjas train.

"*What*?" I accidentally shouted.

The red ninjas in the room immediately snapped their attention to the opening in the wall.

"Whoops," I said, covering my mouth.

"Get them!" Wyatt screamed from the other end of the room. "Don't let them get away!"

I turned around and tried running, but tripped over Gavin's feet. We rolled across the cold floor of the secret passage.

"Get off me!" Gavin shouted.

I pulled myself up. "Sorry about that," I said, helping him to his feet.

Several red ninjas jumped through the opening and started sprinting at us. I pushed Gavin ahead, letting him take the lead again.

"Where's the exit?" Gavin shouted as he ran.

"I don't know!" I replied, keeping an eye on the red ninjas behind us. "Just start turning down random corners! We'll lose these guys and find our way out when it's safe!"

"Turning down random corners doesn't sound safe!"

"Getting beat up by a bunch of ninjas is worse! Trust me!" I shouted.

Gavin darted around one of the dark corners. As I ran toward it, I kicked my foot out, hitting the wall and making a sharp right turn, following my friend as he ran faster.

The red ninjas turned the corner easily and were quickly catching up to us. In the dark passageway, the red from their outfits seemed to glow like charcoal, making them look like monsters tearing through the hall. I felt like I was having a fever dream.

Corner after corner, Gavin ran as I trailed behind him. He

was probably just as scared as I was. As I watched him run, I remembered when he had saved Zoe and me from the red ninjas the first time they chased us. I wasn't sure if we were going to find our way out of this, so I decided the least I could do was give Gavin a shot at escaping. I owed it to him.

When Gavin reached another corner, he turned left. As soon as I made it to the same corner, I turned right. As soon as I did, I dove to the floor and rolled into the edge of the hall, where it was dark enough that it would be difficult to see me.

The red ninjas stopped at the intersection. I saw six of them total.

"Which way did Gavin go?"

"Who cares? It's Chase that we're after!"

"You three go that way, and we'll go this way."

Three of the ninjas punched their chest and yelled, "Ha!" And then they took off down the hall that Gavin had run down. So much for helping him escape.

The other three ninjas stepped into the passage I was in, scanning the corridor for any sign of me. They walked carefully as they approached the spot I was hiding in.

I held my breath to keep myself from giving away my position.

Their sneakers scraped the floor as they stepped right in front of me. I slowly exhaled, keeping as still as possible.

One of the red ninjas stopped. "You hear that?"

His ninja buddy responded. "What?"

Clenching my jaw, I stared at their shoes in front of my face. I could feel a bead of sweat drip down eyelid.

The red ninja pointed his finger down the passageway. "I heard him running! Let's go!"

When the red ninjas were far enough away, I rolled to my feet and dusted my pants off. "Ha!" I said. "Suckers!"

Suddenly a thump came from behind me. When I turned around, I saw four more red ninjas standing in the intersection.

"Spew!" I shouted, instantly taking off.

Footsteps pounded the floor behind me as I ran harder. My side started to ache. I pressed my hand against my ribs as I ran. If I got a cramp at that moment, I'd be dead in the water. My legs were burning, and I had no idea where I was in the school. I guess crawling through a hole in the wall was a bad idea after all!

As hard as I tried, I couldn't do it anymore. My legs, back, and sides were on fire. My gracious sprint had turned into a clumsy stumble as I slid my hand against the cold wall. The passageway was still dark so I couldn't see them, but I could hear the red ninjas huffing and puffing, closing in on me.

Leaning against the wall, I stared down the black hallway I had just been running in, ready to meet my enemy. I pressed my lips together as caught my breath. Closing my eyes, I bumped my head against the wall.

Suddenly, I felt two hands grab my collar and pull on me. That was it. The red ninjas had caught me, but when I opened my eyes, I didn't see anyone in front of me. Instead, I saw a white figure floating above me.

"Huh?" I grunted just before getting yanked into the air. My body flew up high enough to see metal piping along the top of the passageway. I clutched at one of the pipes and pulled myself to safety.

The red ninjas sprinted past me underneath the piping. I watched as they disappeared down the hall.

Catching my breath, I looked to see who my rescuer was, expecting to see an angel robed in white linens. The truth wasn't far from that. Resting on the metal pipes next to me was another ninja, wearing white ninja robes. A full mask covered their whole face, even their eyes. From their size, I could tell they were also a sixth grader.

WHITE NINJA!?

"Who are you?" I whispered.

The white ninja stared at me for a second, silently. And then the kid shrugged his shoulders and dropped to the floor.

I landed on the ground next to him, keeping an eye out for any other red ninjas. Taking a few steps down the passageway, I spoke. "Thanks for saving my butt back there. I would've been dead meat if it hadn't been for—"

When I turned around, the white ninja was gone.

The butterflies in my stomach started flying again as I thought about what had just happened. On top of all the other junk I had to deal with at Buchanan, now I had to add a *white ninja* to the list? Was he a friend or a foe? Wyatt was supposed to be a friend when I first met him, but we all know how *that* turned out.

After a few minutes of walking carefully, I finally found another way out of the passageway. There was an opening that led to the library. All I had to do was remove the cover and walk out. I wouldn't doubt if that secret passage was how Wyatt and red ninjas moved around the school so quickly. If there was an entrance backstage in the cafeteria and in the library, there were sure to be more.

I pulled my ninja mask off just as the bell rang. School was starting and I had no idea where Gavin had run away to. For all I knew, he had been captured by Wyatt and was being held prisoner in that secret room. And the thought of that made my head spin.

Thursday. 10:45 AM. Gym class.

    I had gone back to the cafeteria to look for Gavin after first period, but he wasn't there. Zoe asked if we had caught the penguin. I was sad to tell her no. When she asked where Gavin was, I was sadder to tell her I didn't know.

    I waited in the hallway until the last possible second to see if Gavin would appear, but he never did. Unsure of what to do, I just went to class, hoping things would turn out alright, but I seriously doubted it.

    On the football field, I stood on the sidelines, wearing the dumb moose mask again. I watched as the other students fell in line behind their teams so they could get the game started.

    Jake stepped onto the field, but he didn't approach his team. Instead, he was walking towards me. My face grew warm as I watched him come closer. His wolf pack followed like obedient animals behind him while their red wristbands flopped on their arms.

    When he was a few feet away from me, he stopped, folded his arms, and stared into my mask's eyeholes. "Why even bother wearing the mask anymore?" he asked.

    "Uh, because I'm not on a team, so coach is making me wear it," I replied.

    "No," Jake said, shaking his head. "I mean your *ninja* mask. Why bother wearing it if we all know who you are already."

    I sat there for a moment. "Because *not* everyone knows who I am."

"The kids who matter do," a voice said from behind me.

I turned around and stared through the eyeholes. It was Wyatt. He had found his way to the football field. I looked past him, trying to see if Coach Cooper was outside. He was in his usual spot, reclined in a lawn chair and sipping on lemonade.

As hall monitor captain, Wyatt had a few extra privileges that other students didn't, such as walking the halls whenever he wanted to make sure everyone was in class. Needless to say he was taking advantage of that privilege at that moment.

"We have your friend, you know," Wyatt said. "*Gavin.*"

"Where is he?" I asked, feeling more upset.

Wyatt tugged on his shirtsleeves, refolding them as he spoke. "In a safe place... for *now.*"

"You can't hold kids prisoner," I said. "That's not just something that's frowned upon. I'm pretty sure that's illegal."

Wyatt smiled softly. "I guess the ball's in my court now," he paused, looking at the two football teams on the field. "I mean, in my *possession* now."

I said nothing.

"So how's this sound?" Wyatt started. "You have to do whatever I say or I'll tell Principal Davis *everything* about you."

It felt like the wind had just gotten knocked out of me.

Wyatt grinned. "I'll give you a moment to think about it."

A couple of months ago, Wyatt had stolen my ninja outfit from my book bag. He pulled a series of random crimes while wearing the robes and made sure to get a photo taken of each one. It didn't take long for the school paper to get wind of the story and from there, a ninja in black robes became one of the most wanted students that Buchanan School had ever seen. They never caught Wyatt while he was in my outfit, but hall monitors are still in search of the mysterious ninja.

So you could see how Wyatt telling Principal Davis about my ninja clan wouldn't be the most awesome thing ever... *I* would be the one who got busted for those crimes.

I stared at Wyatt through the holes in the moose mask. I had no doubt that he'd tell Principal Davis about my secret ninja clan. Even though I was framed, I wasn't sure anyone would want to hear my side of the story.

Wyatt chomped on his spearmint gum like a dimwitted

camel. The sloshing sound was unnerving. There he was – the worst bully I'd ever stood before, threatening to tell on me.

I shook my head at him. There was no way I was gonna go down like that. He had power and he was trying to hold it over my head like a balloon filled with water. If I made him upset, he'd pop the balloon and soak me to my skin.

But then a crazy thing happened in my head. I blinked a couple times, collecting my thoughts, and suddenly everything became clear to me.

All I had to do was take that power away from him.

I chuckled as the realization hit me like a bag of oranges. He said he'd give me a moment to think about it, but all I needed was a millisecond.

I pushed the moose mask off my head, dropping it to the ground with a thick thud sound. I heard most of the gym class gasp when they realized it was me in the costume, but I didn't really care. Spinning in place, I began marching across the field, back to the school.

"Wait," Wyatt muttered. "What're you doing? Where are you going?"

"To tell Principal Davis *myself*," I shouted.

I could hear Wyatt's voice panic as he spoke to Jake and his crew. "Is he serious? He's going to go to the principal? That's madness! Is he crazy?"

My smile stretched wider across my face.

Wyatt's footsteps beat against the grassy field as he caught up to me. Cutting me off, he held his hands up. "Fine, dude! You win! We *don't* have Gavin prisoner anywhere! Just don't go to Davis and tell him everything, okay?"

I stopped walking. "What do you mean you *don't* have Gavin?"

Wyatt caught his breath, reluctant to tell me the truth. Finally, he clenched his eyes shut and gave up. "My ninjas couldn't find him after you two split up. He totally got away from us, alright? I was *lying* to you to get you to do what I wanted. You called my bluff, happy? Gavin's in class right now – fit as a fiddle – snug as a bug – cozy as a cat! Whatever term makes you most comfortable! He's fine!"

I looked Wyatt in the eye. I could tell he was being honest because he looked more worried than angry. "How do you know he's in class?" I asked.

Wyatt put his hands on his hips and glared at me. "I'm the hall monitor captain, remember? I checked on him after the bell rang. He didn't even look fazed."

For about two seconds, I forgot that Wyatt was the bad guy. Then it all came back to me. I stepped forward, tapping my finger against his chest. "Principal Davis has no clue about you or your ninjas, does he? That's why you were freaked when I said I was gonna tell him everything myself!"

"Of course he doesn't!" Wyatt said sternly. "Are you nuts?"

I stepped past the leader of the red ninja clan and continued toward the locker rooms. Gym wasn't over, but I already had all the exercise I could handle for that day. Coach Cooper wouldn't let me out of class until it was over, but I knew he wouldn't mind if I took it easy right next to him. Maybe he had an extra glass of lemonade.

"Chase!" Wyatt shouted.

I spun around, waiting for him to speak.

"We're ninjas," he said. "And we live by a code, you and I. It's like the bro-code, but with ninjas."

"And what's that?" I asked. "I thought the bro-code meant you couldn't date your friend's ex-girlfriend or something."

"Okay, it's nothing like the bro-code then," Wyatt admitted. "The point is that I'd never tell anyone about your secret identity, and I'd hope you'd do the same for me. I bluffed when I said I'd tell Principal Davis, but you should know it was an empty threat."

I was confused. "Why are you telling me this?"

"Because I feel like I owe it to you," Wyatt explained. "That's at least one thing you can be sure about of me."

Wyatt turned in place and hiked back to the football field. I chewed my lip, confused about what had just happened. Since the beginning of the school year, Wyatt had been nothing but trouble for me. Was it possible that maybe he was starting to let up a little? From my experience with him, the answer should've been no, but everyone deserves a second chance...

Don't they?

Thursday. 11:30 AM. Lunch.

When I got to the front doors of the cafeteria, I couldn't find Gavin anywhere. Maybe it was because I had been a few minutes late everyday since I wanted to meet with my ninja clan, but with our secret base getting hijacked by Wyatt, we were without a home.

Several kids from my ninja clan were already in the cafeteria wearing their normal street clothes. I nodded to them as I walked through the doors, feeling a bit sheepish at having lost our base for a *second* time since becoming their leader. I wish I could tell them I had a plan to fix everything, but the truth was that I didn't.

Because of the week I'd had, I felt exhausted and stretched thin, like a drop of syrup trying to cover a stack of pancakes.

After a minute of walking aimlessly, I saw Gavin sitting at a table with Zoe and Faith. I was happy to see that Gavin wasn't a prisoner somewhere in the dungeon of the school. I dragged my feet across the ground to meet my friends.

"You look tired," Faith said when she noticed me.

"I am," I replied, taking a seat next to her.

"Well, you can take it easy," Zoe said. "We haven't been able to find Calvin anywhere in here."

I looked around the cafeteria. I wasn't surprised to see that a lot of the other sixth graders were missing. It wasn't like it was totally empty, but it was at least empty enough that even a few of the teachers standing against the wall had started to notice.

104

"You know where this kid probably is?" I asked, feeling a pit in my stomach at the thought of the red ninjas secret green house training room.

Gavin nodded, but didn't say anything. I didn't either because I didn't want to freak out Zoe or Faith.

"Where?" Zoe asked. "In fact, it seems like a bunch of kids have been absent this week, hasn't it?"

Faith shrugged a shoulder. "Just during lunch," she said. "All my classes have been full, which is weird because the cafeteria seems so vacant."

I kept quiet, fully knowing that the missing kids were training as red ninjas.

Zoe turned her body, trying to peer through the tinted glass walls of the cafeteria so she could see the library, which was directly on the other side of the hall. "They better not be in the library! I'd *hate* if that room got flooded with a bunch of students! I'd *never* find a seat."

"Doubt it," Faith joked. "Maybe the cafeteria is just getting larger?"

I stood from the table. "I'm gonna take a look around," I said somberly as I started to walk away from the table.

Gavin started to get up, but I raised my hand. "It's cool," I said. "I just want to be alone for now."

Dropping back into his chair, Gavin faced Zoe and Faith again. I could hear their jokes as I walked farther down the aisle. I hoped their feelings weren't hurt. It wasn't that I wanted to be apart from them. It was that I actually needed to be in my own head.

All of the talent show gear was set up, waiting to be used on Friday, which was less than twenty-four hours from that moment. Without being able to find Calvin, I had an awful feeling that he was going to pull some prank during the show, wrecking it for everyone. It was so weird trying to picture it all happening because in my mind, Calvin's face was blank since I didn't know who he was or what he even looked like.

I knew that if I wanted to find Calvin, I could start with the green house. The only thing about that was that it'd be *filled* with members of the red ninja clan, and I probably wouldn't make it out without at least one black eye as a souvenir.

"Mister Chase Cooper!" said a boy's voice from behind me.

I spun in place, looking at the kid who said my name. I was a bit taken back when I recognized him. "President Sebastian?"

PRESIDENT SEBASTIAN

Sebastian held his open hand out to me. He was dressed in a fancy light gray suit with a red striped necktie. Standing behind him were two other boys in suits, both wearing aviator sunglasses and occasionally tossing a glance over their shoulders. "Pleased to finally meet you," the president said.

I took his hand, gripped it tightly, and shook it like I was in a business meeting. "Likewise," I said.

Grasping my hand firmly, the president yanked me close enough so he could whisper. "I *know* you were back in the greenhouse yesterday. I know it was *you*."

I pulled my hand away from the president's hold. "So what?" I said, frustrated and suddenly angry that Sebastian was *not* there to make peace. "I'm sure Wyatt filled you in on *all* the details, didn't he?"

Sebastian tugged at his coat sleeve. "No," he said. "Wyatt never said a word about you. It was his cousin, Carlyle."

"What's Carlyle got to do with it?" I asked, and then I

realized I actually had no clue what was happening at all. "No, wait. Start way back from the beginning. What's your deal with Wyatt? Why'd you give him the position of hall monitor captain?"

"Doesn't Wyatt deserve it?" Sebastian asked softly, as if my questions were irrelevant.

I was so shocked that I had to lift my jaw off the floor. "No," I said firmly. "He *doesn't* deserve it! You're planning something, and I *know* it."

"Oh, do you?" Sebastian asked, folding his arms.

"Well, no," I said, "but I *assume* that you are... since everything that you've done has been shady."

"Welcome to the *real* world," Sebastian laughed. His face suddenly tightened and grew angry. He glared at me and said, "Not that you can do anything to stop us now, but you best mind your business, *son*. Or else you're *done*. 'Cause we've already *won*."

I about cracked up because he sounded like a children's rhyming book. "Yeah? Was it *fun*? When you *won* under the *sun* tanning yo' *buns*?"

Sebastian's face flushed with anger. He pointed at me one last time. "Just stay out of our way, or you'll be sorry!"

The two hall monitors stepped aside, allowing President Sebastian to walk through them. I watched as they used the kitchen doors to exit the cafeteria instead of the doors at the front of the room.

I *knew* that kid was up to something, but now I *really* knew it. Unfortunately I didn't know *what* kind of plan he was scheming. I doubted that it had anything to do with the talent show since Sebastian's shady actions had started long before Zoe had even talked about putting it on.

Staring at the back of the stage, I thought about the white ninja that had saved me from getting my butt handed to me in a doggy bag. Was he a good guy or a bad guy? Since he helped me get away, I could only *hope* he was on *my* side.

Friday. 8:00 AM. The talent show.

Finally, the day of the talent show had arrived, and everyone was in high spirits. Zoe was running around like a superhero as she supervised every little detail of the show.

Students were lined up on the stage, reading sheets of paper that probably had the schedule for the morning. The stage that Gavin had fixed looked awesome and solid as a rock. In fact, if I didn't know the corner was busted earlier in the week, I'd never be able to tell.

Overnight, a crew had set up a few hundred foldout chairs, lining them in rows for the audience. The cafeteria lights had been switched off, and the talent show stage lights were being tested, making the room look like some sort of dance club.

The only students in the cafeteria were those who had acts in the show. Everyone was standing around, laughing and having a good time. It actually felt relieving to see others enjoying themselves. The missing penguin had been in everyone's thoughts all week, but nobody knew that Hotcakes might've been just the tip of the iceberg.

The rest of the sixth graders at Buchanan would arrive when homeroom dismissed, which was still about twenty minutes away. The first half of the school day had been dedicated to Zoe's talent show, which was killer because it meant all those classes would be put on hold, but it also meant the last half of the day's classes would be put on hold too, replaced with a three hour outdoor lunch. The entire day was basically a free day.

Gavin was sitting on the edge of the stage so I had to weave between students to get to him. Just beyond the stage curtain, I saw several different props for different acts.

Some bright blue flying discs caught my eye right away. My dad played a lot of disc golf, which is how I recognized the small circular toys, but the discs on the stage were extra cool because they had a four-pointed star logo printed on their face that reminded me of ninja stars.

I heard Zoe's voice nearby. "I don't understand why that scaffolding is even in here still!" she growled. "You know how much of an eyesore that is?"

Looking to my left, I saw my cousin venting some frustration to Gavin and Faith.

"When people look back on this day, all they're gonna think of is that *ugly* scaffolding!" Zoe said as she pointed to the metal cage above the bench on the wall. "Look! Even those orange paint cans have been left on top of it!"

Gavin patted the air, which I think was becoming his signature move. "Relax," he said calmly. "I'll find Adam and figure it all out. You just worry about the talent show."

Zoe held up her clipboard. "I'm sorry," she said. "I just got a lot of stuff to do before the show starts, which is in about twenty minutes." And then she looked over at me. "Oh, good! You're here! Could you do me a favor?"

"Of course," I said.

Zoe pointed to a couple of foldup chairs leaning against the front of the stage. "Could you take those backstage? We've got enough chairs out here so those are extra."

I wrapped my hands around the two chairs, surprised that they were actually pretty heavy. As I lifted them up, I played it off like it was no big deal. Smiling a little too wide, I struggled to speak. "No problemo!"

Zoe returned to her clipboard and walked to the back of the cafeteria. Gavin and Faith followed, waiting for instructions on what they could do to help.

After I took the chairs backstage, I leaned them against the wall. Opening and closing my fists, I tried to squeeze the pain out of them, even making the "*sssssssssss*," sound, sucking in air through my teeth.

And that's when I saw him. Hotcakes was poking his head out from the small opening in the wall again.

"Seriously?" I asked, frustrated at the penguin. As I slowly approached it, I spoke softly. "There's no way I'm gonna scream your name while I'm back here so please just let me *grab* your tiny little bird body…"

Hotcakes torqued his head, gazing at my hands that were reaching for him. The penguin jerked its body, shuddering like it was cold, but it didn't move.

"Gooooooood birdie," I sang. "Gooooooooood biiiiiiiirdie."

Hotcakes hopped forward and hissed at me.

I flinched, reeling my hands back in, and scolded the penguin through my clenched teeth. "You're being a *bad* penguin! You know that? *Bad* penguin!"

Instead of running back into the opening in the wall, Hotcakes darted deeper into the backstage area, zooming like a tiny missile.

Glancing over my shoulder, I considered calling out for help, but decided against it. It was still early in the morning so the red ninjas were sure to be training in the greenhouse outside just beyond the small opening in the wall. I couldn't risk them hearing me shout for help.

I swiftly walked backstage, following Hotcakes. "Heeeeeeere, Hotcaaaaaaakes," I whispered. "Heeeeeeere, little frustrating bird that has wings, but can't fly."

Cardboard boxes shook slightly against the walls, one after the other. Reminding myself that Sophia said the penguin was perfectly safe and wouldn't bite, I continued to follow it through the cramped path backstage.

I kept my distance, watching as the hidden penguin bumped into different boxes and hanging costumes. If I didn't know it was a penguin, I would've been freaked out that I had just found a ghost. Every few seconds, the penguin would dash across the narrow corridor, disturbing all the junk on the other side.

As I made it to the end of the line, where the hallway narrowed enough that it was impossible to keep going forward, I stopped. The short stack of cardboards boxes against the end of the corridor jostled, and then suddenly stopped.

"What?" I asked out loud, confused. Slowly moving my foot forward, I slid the short stack of cardboard boxes out of the way.

On the other side of the boxes, where I thought the backstage had ended, was a thin metal door that was pushed open about six inches. The penguin must've gone into the next room.

I opened the door all the way and found a set of stairs. It wasn't a full flight of steps as you'd expect, but only half that. I wasn't surprised to see Hotcakes at the top, peeking out at me almost mockingly.

Steadily, I stepped one foot over the other without taking my eyes off the penguin. But as the rest of the room came into view, I almost forgot the bird was even there.

You know that point in a movie when the hero suddenly makes a life changing discovery? Like, the camera shows them walking over a small rocky hill as a massive background reveals itself, and the orchestra music starts slowly swelling until the camera swings around and shows you the shocked look on the hero's face. That's when the drums start pounding in the background, and it's almost like the hero has been transformed...

Yeah, *that's* how it felt as I walked up those dirty steps.

At the top of the half staircase, the room had completely opened up. It was so large that I felt tiny standing in the middle of it all. Each step I took, my sneakers squished on the ground. When I looked down, I saw that I was walking on wrestling mats that covered the entire floor.

The walls were cinder blocks with flags hanging from them. Each flag represented a year that Buchanan School had won a wrestling tournament. The last flag on the far end of the room had the year 1999 on it.

If the red ninjas weren't training in there, then it meant they didn't know it even existed. Ideas started racing through my mind of how awesome it would be if my ninja clan had a place like that to train in.

I heard a chirp at my feet. When I looked down, Hotcakes was nestling his body against my calf. I almost asked the penguin if it had brought me there on purpose, but decided not to because that idea was crazy. But a small part of me couldn't shake the idea that maybe he had.

Carefully, I reached down and wrapped my hands around Hotcakes. The penguin didn't try to get free, allowing me to pick him up.

Another door across the room creaked open. Coach Cooper stepped through and walked over to the light switch on the wall. He stopped when he noticed me. "Chase?" he asked. "What're you doing—" he paused, pointing at the bird in my hands. "You found the penguin!"

"I did!" I laughed.

"Did you follow it in here?" Coach Cooper asked.

"Yeah," I said. "It came in through the door down the steps."

The gym teacher nodded. "Nice work, kiddo. Sophia will be glad to hear it, but probably not as much as Principal Davis." The coach continued to the light switch on the wall and flipped the lights off. He gestured to the stairs I had walked up. "Go back that way and shut the door, would ya?"

I started to turn around, but paused, remembering my ninja clan was without a home. "Hey, coach?" I said.

Coach Cooper turned around in the doorway. "Yeah?"

"What's the deal with this room?"

Leaning against the frame of the exit, Coach Cooper spoke reminiscently. "Back in the day, we used to have a wrestling team, but the program was cut due to funding. This room is all that's left from that."

"So it's not being used for anything?" I asked, hugging the penguin in my arms.

The coach sighed. "Sometimes it's used for gymnastics week, but for the rest of the year, it's locked up."

"Is it something I could use?" I asked immediately. "I mean, if I started some kind of athletic club or something?"

"Don't suppose why not," the coach said, scanning the room. "It's empty like this all the time. The only requirement is that the wrestling mats have to be cleaned daily if you're going to use the room."

That was a small price to pay for a full sized training arena. "No problem," I said, smiling.

The coach pointed at the stairs behind me again. "Get back out to the talent show, Chase. We can discuss these details after that, but just so I know, what kind of *athletic* club do you want to start?"

I paused, trying to think of a good answer. I didn't want to say I was going to use it for ninja training, but I also didn't want to lie. "Martial arts," I said finally.

"Cool," Coach Cooper said, tossing a thumbs-up at me. Then he waved. "Back to the talent show!"

I didn't hesitate. I spun around and jumped down the steps, clearing all of them in one leap. Hotcakes didn't seem to mind.

After exiting the secret wrestling room, I pushed the short stack of boxes back against the thin metal door. I didn't want to risk Wyatt or any members of his red ninja clan finding it.

The noise from all the kids preparing for the talent show flooded the backstage area, so I wasn't worried about anyone hearing me. As I marched down the narrow corridor, I found the cage that Hotcakes had escaped from. Gently, I set the penguin back into it, and shut the metal gate, locking the latch.

"Sorry, Hotcakes," I said. "But I think it's best if I keep you in here while I find Sophia."

The penguin chirped at me.

Jogging back to the cafeteria, I hopped from the backstage and onto the lunchroom floor. Zoe was still running back and forth between her crew, barking orders at them. Along the wall, I saw

114

most of the students in the talent show sitting on the bench, waiting their turn. Eli and Sophia were the first two students on the bench.

I was just about to shout for Sophia until someone grabbed at my shirt collar with two hands and pulled me aside. It was Adam who clutched at my shirt. Gavin was standing right behind him. "What're you doing?" I asked, upset that my shirt was getting stretched out.

Adam's eyes were wide as he spoke frantically. "I saw *Calvin* outside in the lobby!" he said. "I overheard him say something about messing with the stage again!"

Gavin stepped closer. "We gotta find him before he does anything!"

"We should go to Principal Davis about this, shouldn't we?" I suggested.

"There's no time!" Adam said. "You have to go out there and stop him!"

Feeling a little panicked at that point, I said, "But we don't even know what this kid looks like!"

"He's wearing an orange shirt with stripes!" Adam said, pushing me toward the cafeteria doors.

"Alright, fine!" I said. "Just let go of me!"

Gavin pulled open the door and left the lunchroom first. I followed, pressing the fabric of my collar down, trying to undo the damage Adam had done. For some reason, there were tiny pink and green threads all over my shirt, probably from Adam when he grabbed me. It was annoying having to wipe them all off. I knew I had seen that style thread before, but I couldn't remember where.

I was so distracted that I didn't even notice Wyatt trying to enter the room. Staring at my shirt, I jumped forward, accidently knocking against Wyatt. He fell into the cafeteria door and bounced to the ground. A cup of water spilled down the front of his outfit.

"*Really?*" Wyatt shouted, angry.

I stepped over the leader of the red ninjas and chuckled. "Sorry, man!" I said, and honestly, I *was* sorry because it was an accident. "Seriously, I didn't mean to do that!"

"You soaked my shirt!" Wyatt shouted. "Where are you going? Get *back* here!"

I slipped into the crowd of students, following Gavin. If I had stayed to let Wyatt yell at me, I know the situation would've just gotten worse. Even though I didn't want to, I knew I'd find him later to apologize because it actually *was* my fault.

The lobby of the school was so full of sixth graders that it was almost impossible to move. As Gavin pushed himself through the crowd, I did my best to stay as close to him as possible.

"You see him?" Gavin asked over the noisy crowd.

"A kid with an orange shirt?" I asked. "Nope."

Gavin zigzagged through the students, checking each t-shirt. Then he stopped, and shouted, "Calvin? Does anyone know a Calvin?"

The crowd of students ignored the question, except for the few girls nearby that shot dirty looks at Gavin for yelling in their ears.

I clutched the back of Gavin's shirt so I wouldn't lose him. "There's no way we're gonna find him in all this," I said. "This is hopeless!"

"We can't just give up," Gavin replied.

"What if we stood by the doors and checked everyone's shirt as they entered the cafeteria?" I suggested.

"We need to find him *before* he gets in there," Gavin said. "We can't risk him sabatoguing the stage—"

Abruptly, Gavin stopped talking and darted forward, grabbing another student's elbow.

When he pulled the student closer, I saw the orange shirt with stripes. It *had* to be the kid Adam talked about! It *had* to be Calvin!

Gavin's face twisted out of anger. "It's over, Calvin! We *know* what you're planning!"

The boy in Gavin's grip looked confused. "What? What're you talking about? *Who's Calvin?*"

I paused. "*You are.*"

The boy whipped his arms out, escaping Gavin's grip. "No, I'm not! My name is Max!"

Principal Davis suddenly appeared next to us, as if he somehow teleported to that spot. "What's the problem here? Gavin? Chase? What're you two doing?"

Gavin spoke quickly, trying to defend himself. "We were

trying to stop Calvin from—"

The principal interrupted him. "Calvin?" he asked, confused.

"Yeah," I said, pointing at the kid in the orange shirt. "His name is *Calvin*... we *think*."

"Nooooo," Principal Davis said, shaking his head. "This boy's name is Max."

Max folded his arms and stared daggers at me.

And then the principal said something that totally blew my mind. "There's *nobody* at this school named Calvin. Trust me, I would know since that's my first name too."

My jaw about hit the floor. What Principal Davis said couldn't be possible could it? We had spent the entire week searching for someone named *Calvin*. Sophia, Eli, and Adam *all* said they saw *Calvin* messing with the penguin cage and the stage. That name had come up in more than a couple conversations, and now the principal was telling us he didn't exist?

I felt an itch on the front of my neck from where Adam had left all those tiny pink and green threads. When I scratched it, I suddenly remembered where I had seen those threads. It was the same pink and green that was on the rope tied to the scaffolding. The same scaffolding that had paint cans nailed to the top of it. The same scaffolding that was still in the lunchroom, looming over the heads of all the talent show contestants.

All the contestants *except* for Sophia and Eli.

My eye twitched. There was so many dots connecting in my mind that I was scared my head would burst like fire cracker.

I spun around and ran back to the cafeteria windows. Cupping my hands on the tinted glass, I squinted so I could see clearly.

Adam was messing around backstage. He was alone, and I could see that the braided rope was in his hands. For some reason he had the rope wound around his fists while he tugged lightly at it.

I followed the rope with my eyes. It was partially hidden because of the stage curtain that hung in front of it, which was why it was barely noticeable. On the other side of the curtain, along the cafeteria floor, the rope trailed all the way back to the bench along the wall, where it curved upward and was tied off to the wooden plank on top of the scaffolding, which coincidentally, *hadn't* been

118

removed from the cafeteria yet.

On top of the plank, I saw the orange paint cans that had been nailed into place, but there were more cans up there than at the beginning of the week, and I could tell that they had been opened because the lids had been popped out.

Every student in the talent show had taken their place along the bench, and they were all seated *under* the scaffolding, except for Sophia and Eli, who were just on the other side of the metal cage, *safe* from the paint cans above.

My mouth felt dry as I realized that one good tug from Adam, and the plank with the paint cans would flip over, dumping paint all over the kids in the talent show, *except* for Sophia and Eli.

"Good gravy," I whispered.

Those three had been playing us since the beginning of the week!

I pushed my way through the crowd and jumped back into the cafeteria. I wasn't sure if Gavin was behind me or not, but I couldn't waste any time to check.

Glancing at the clock, I saw that there were still a few

minutes until it was 8:20, the official start time of the talent show. Everyone had taken their places along the bench on the wall. Zoe was back at the soundboard, making final adjustments to the speaker system. Gavin was still in the lobby, Faith was nowhere to be seen, and neither was Brayden.

Sneaking along the wall, I climbed the steps to the backstage and scanned the area. Adam was hidden behind the curtain on the opposite side of the stage, holding the braided rope in his hands. When was he going to pull it?

"Places everyone!" Zoe's voice said over the speakers. "The show starts... *now!*"

I stared at Adam from across the stage as I listened to all the sixth graders in the school pour into the cafeteria. The sounds of conversation and laughter filled the air as chairs scraped against the linoleum floor of the lunchroom. If I ran across the stage at that moment, I was sure to get noticed, which would lead to Adam freaking out and pulling the rope, so I waited, thinking of what my next move should be.

And then at that moment, something nailed my back, knocking me to the floor. The stage curtain had been pushed to the side, blocking anyone from seeing me.

"Our leader thinks you oughta be punished for getting his shirt wet!" said a raspy voice.

When I rolled over, I saw five members of the red ninjas standing over me. Wonderful, I thought. This day was just getting worse and worse.

"How 'bout we do this another time?" I said, rising from the floor. "Wyatt can play bully all he wants on Monday, I promise, just so long as you guys leave me alone right now."

The red ninja in front shot his foot out at me. Obviously they weren't going to listen. I tried dodging the attack, but it struck me right in the chest. The force from the kick knocked me backward. As I stumbled over my feet, I knew I was going to land out in the open in front of everyone. In order to keep anyone from recognizing me, I pulled my ninja mask over my head.

When I was finally able to stop myself, I was in the middle of the talent show stage, in front of every sixth grader in the school. I rose from the floor slowly, as everyone's eyes stared at me. Hushed whispers filtered through the room about the ninja on stage.

I thought for sure the red ninjas would keep themselves hidden, but they boldly stepped out into the open and formed a circle around me. I couldn't believe what was happening. Were these guys really looking for a fight? On a stage? In front of the entire school?

One of the red ninjas balled his fists and pointed them at me. "S'up, *nerdling*," his voice said from behind his mask.

I studied the ninja's eyes. "Jake," I whispered.

"You embarrassed me on the field," Jake said. "So now it's time for a little payback."

Remaining in place, I watched as the four other red ninjas slowly started circling me. My heart started racing as I looked out into the room. Principal Davis was standing at the back just *watching* what was happening! *Why wasn't anyone trying to stop this?*

My eyes scanned the room until I made eye contact with my cousin. She was back by the soundboard, glaring at me with her arms crossed. I had no doubt that she knew it was me on the stage, dressed in a black ninja outfit.

Jake turned, punched his fist into his open palm, and bowed to the crowd. Everyone clapped their hands, eager for the show to start, and then I realized *that* was why nobody was doing anything – because they thought it was part of the show!

I sunk my body down on one foot and raised my open hands in front of me, taking a defensive stance. I stared at the open space in front of me, allowing my eyes to relax so I could see everything by looking at nothing. It was the same ninja technique I had used a couple days before, when I was searching backstage for Hotcakes.

I've said it a million times before, but I'm against fighting. I won't throw a punch even if one is thrown at me. Faith helped me realized that a couple months ago at the skating party. The second I throw a punch, I just become another kid who got in a fight at school. Standing up to bullies meant that I couldn't bring myself down to their level – and *fighting* a stupid fight would've done just that. I'm Chase Cooper, and I *knew* I was better than that.

Orange spotlights started pulsing on and off. Apparently the kid by the light board thought he'd try and make things look cooler. I'm sure to the audience it did, but it was a little distracting for me.

The tallest of the red ninjas threw a couple of intimidation lunges at me while saying, "*What? You want some? What now, huh? What?*"

I had to look up because the ninja was so tall. They must've been the same height as an adult, but there was *no way* any *teachers* in the school were in Wyatt's red ninja clan. And then I remembered that there *was* that one student at Buchanan that was, like, seven feet tall. It was probably her.

Jake jumped at me first, spinning in the air, and launching a kick right for my head. I trusted that my reflexes would respond because I knew if I thought about it too hard, I'd freeze up and get pummeled. It worked perfectly.

I casually stepped to the side, dodging Jake's attack as he sailed past me. Two of the red ninjas in front came at me at the same time, throwing fists in the air like they just didn't care. I put my hands behind my back and leaned to the side, dodging both punches like it was my job. I even added a sarcastic remark. "Thanks for the offer, but I think I'll pass on your punches today."

Spinning in place, I faced all five of the red ninjas. I kept my hands behind my back because I didn't want to accidently throw a punch without thinking. Honestly, I felt like some sort of old wise ninja guru playing with a bunch of kids.

I had to smile under my mask. I think it was obvious because of how my eyes looked.

Jake ran forward, screaming some sort of battle cry. I shifted my feet so my body twisted sideways, blocking his punch with my elbow. Frustrated, Jake tossed out a fury of jabs. I leaned away from most of the attacks. The rest I continued to block with my elbow. The craziest part about it was that time slowed down as it all happened. After each attack, I watched as he slowly dragged his arm through space, giving me enough time to just step away from it.

The sixth graders in the crowd cheered each time I dodged an attack. They had no idea that I was in the middle of an actual fight, but they probably wouldn't have cared since nobody was actually landing any hits.

Several of the red ninjas ran toward me at the same time, a few taking the high road, while the rest took the low. I leaned over and spun on my feet, letting the ninjas kick at the air above me. When they were past, I continued my spin, raising one of my knees to avoid a low spinning sweep at my legs.

I was feeling good, better than I ever had in my life, but that came to an end pretty quickly. When I turned to face the ninjas, Jake was already diving toward me with his body. I tried to move out of the way, but it was too late.

I felt Jake's shoulder smash into me, forcing me to the ground. Everyone in the cafeteria gasped, probably shocked because the attack looked and sounded so real. What they didn't know was that it *was* real.

Tasting blood in my mouth, I set my knee on the ground and looked up just in time to see Jake coming in for his finishing move. Lifting my arms, I blocked my face, but instead of feeling pain, I felt a rush of air blast through me, and then a loud "*whoomph*" sound.

I heard Jake's muffled voice shouting. When I opened my eyes, he wasn't standing in front of me anymore. Instead, I was staring at the mysterious white ninja. He was standing like a superhero on top of a small mountain of red velvet that looked like that curtain. And then I realized it *was* the curtain.

The white ninja had dropped the stage curtain on the red ninjas in order to save me! The white ninja *was* on my side!

"Who are you?" I asked from the floor.

The white ninja turned toward me, his mask fully covering his entire face. With a low growl, the white ninja spoke, obviously disguising his voice. "A friend," he said.

Spinning in a circle, the white ninja threw a small pouch at the floor. It popped, instantly creating a white cloud of chalk dust. When the dust cleared, the white ninja was gone.

"*Awesome!*" I whispered.

The school burst with applause, thinking it was part of the act. Everyone stood to their feet, shouting loudly, completely clueless about the reality of what had happened.

I shook my head, clearing my thoughts. Scooting to the back of the stage, I took my ninja mask off, looking once more at the pile of red ninjas as they struggled under the red velvet curtain.

I blinked, glancing across the room and saw Adam. His jaw was dropped open as he stared at the curtain too, but his hand was still gripping the rope attached to the scaffolding.

I stepped forward, accidently catching his attention. His eyebrows furrowed as his eyes flashed with rage. Grasping the rope with both hands, he yanked it to the side, pulling it tight.

My eyes darted to scaffolding above the talent show participants. I watched as the plank of wood, along with the paint cans, started tipping over.

Frantically, I searched the stage for anything that could help me, and saw the flying discs used for the disc golf act. I dove across the stage, grabbing one of the discs with the four-pointed star logo. Spinning my arm out wide, I flung the disc as hard as I could at the spot above the contestants.

Everyone in the room was still busy cheering for the ninja performance that they didn't notice what was happening. I watched with eyes wide open as they disc flew across the room.

The plank continued to tip farther and farther until finally...

CRANK!

The flying disc lodged itself into the corner of the plank, where the wood met the scaffolding, jamming tightly into place. The four-pointed star logo stuck out like a ninja star. The paint cans spilled a couple drops of paint over their rims, but nothing fell from the scaffolding. The kids in the talent show were safe!

"Ha!" I shouted, raising a fist into the air.

Adam dropped the rope and ran down the side of the stage. He hopped to the floor and headed toward one of the side doors of the cafeteria. Kicking the exit open, he jumped out. Sophia and Eli bolted from their place on the bench and ran out the door too.

Gavin sprinted across the back of the room, jumping over empty metal chairs. Zoe started to follow him, but stopped herself when she remembered she had a talent show to put on. I leapt off the stage and joined Gavin at the exit where the three suspects had escaped. Without saying a word, Gavin pushed open the door and together we stepped through.

On the other side of the door, I was expecting another chase through the halls of Buchanan School. Needless to say I was pleasantly surprised when I found out it wasn't necessary.

Adam, Sophia, and Eli were in the middle of an argument in the empty hallway.

"*My* fault?" Sophia shouted. "*You* were the one who said Hotcakes wouldn't be out of his cage for more than a minute! He's been missing all week!"

"The plan was *working*!" Adam shouted defensively. "If you had just stuck to the original plan, we would've gotten away with *all* of this!"

Principal Davis and Coach Cooper stepped through the cafeteria doors and into the hall. The principal folded his arms and shook his head.

Adam pointed down the hallway and suddenly had a frightened look upon his face. "There! The kid who set Sophia's penguin loose ran that way! If you hurry, you can catch him!"

Sophia's face grew bright red, and if she were a cartoon

character, I'm sure steam would've shot out of her ears. "That's enough!" she shouted. "I've had *enough* of this lying and cheating!"

Adam waved his hands around and opened his eyes wide at Sophia. "You're just frustrated, that's all! You've lost your penguin and are just having an *angry* moment, okay? We should all just calm down and count to—"

"No!" Sophia said. "I'm *done* with this! I played along all week, but I'm *done* now! *None* of this is worth it!"

Principal Davis spoke sternly. "*Someone* tell me what this is all about."

"This is about Adam cheating so we could win the talent show!" Sophia said.

Adam began stumbling over his words as he tried to defend himself.

Sophia spoke louder so Adam couldn't. She pointed at him and revealed the entire scheme. "Adam's been planning on dumping paint all over the other kids in the talent show!"

"I *knew* it!" I shouted, hopping in the air once.

Everyone looked at me.

I kicked at the floor, embarrassed.

Sophia continued. "Adam rigged the scaffolding above everyone so that he could yank a rope to tip the wooden plank over on top. The paint cans were nailed to the wood so that the cans themselves wouldn't fall off and actually cause harm."

"Come on!" Adam said. "That doesn't even sound like something a kid would do! I mean, really? Scheme a diabolical plan? Bah!"

"You *did* it and you *know* it!" Sophia said, angry. "After the paint would drop on everyone, there would only be two students left in the talent show – *Eli* and *me*. Since we would be the last two contestants, it didn't matter which one of us won because we'd all split the thousand dollar grand prize three ways. Three hundred and thirty bucks to each of us, with the remaining ten dollars going to buy ice cream cones to celebrate."

"So the penguin was your part, and Adam was supposed to pull the rope," Principal Davis said, "but what about Eli? What's his role in all this?"

Sophia pressed her lips together. "It was Eli's job to set

Hotcakes free on Monday, which he did."

"*You* were the kid in the hockey mask?" Gavin asked Eli.

Eli paused, but caved under the pressure. "Yes," he whispered. "My job was to open the cage and run, creating a diversion, so Adam could pull the rope. Everyone was supposed to get splashed with orange paint during Monday morning's rehearsal."

"So what happened?" Gavin asked. "Your plan wasn't successful at all."

"Well, the rope didn't work on Monday," Eli said. "It wasn't tied tight enough."

"And the broken stage?" Gavin said.

"That was just an accident," Eli admitted. "I banged into it as I was racing out of the room."

"So the broken stage wasn't even supposed to happen?" I asked.

Eli shook his head.

"Why didn't Sophia just set her own penguin free?" Gavin asked.

Sophia spoke again. "Adam said it would be less obvious if someone *other* than the penguin's owner set it free. That way I'd still be in the cafeteria worried sick about Hotcakes."

"Wait wait wait," Gavin said, holding his palms up. "So who's *Calvin?*"

"Calvin doesn't exist!" Sophia said. "If anyone suspected anything, we were all supposed to blame a kid named Calvin so that everyone in the school would go looking for *him* instead of the real criminals."

"Clever," I whispered.

"So that's where you messed up," Gavin said. "You told us Eli had something to do with it on Monday."

"You *what?*" Adam shouted. "*You didn't tell them Calvin's name?*"

Sophia's eyes grew fierce. "I *did* tell them Calvin's name, but it was *after* I already said Eli's name on accident! I couldn't think straight because Hotcakes was actually missing! This whole week has been a disaster for me and you know what? I regret the entire thing!" She looked back at Principal Davis and spoke again. "None of this was worth the trouble, and I shouldn't have gone along with it. Hotcakes could be anywhere by now and it's all my fault for playing along with this dumb idea."

I stepped forward with a smug look on my face. "I think you'll be happy to hear that Hotcakes is back in his cage backstage," I said.

Sophia let out a long gasp as her eyes widened. She looked at me with the biggest puppy dog eyes I'd ever seen. *Really? He's back in his cage and safe?*

I nodded. "Yup," I said, and then I started telling her about how I was the one who found her penguin, but the principal interrupted me.

"We can sort all this out when your parents get here," Principal Davis said, gesturing the three guilty students to walk to his office. "For now, I'm just glad this is over."

Sophia punched Adam's arm as they walked away. "You just better be glad Hotcakes is alright! I love that stinkin' bird with all my heart and if anything happened to him, it'd be the *end* of you."

Principal Davis glanced at Coach Cooper. Both of them shook their head at each other as they escorted the students back to the office.

Gavin and I watched everyone walk away until they disappeared around the corner. He turned back toward me and laughed victoriously. I couldn't help but laugh too.

"Wow," Gavin said. "I can't believe they all just gave each other up like that!"

"To be fair," I said, "Adam *tried* to keep the lie going."

Wiping his hands together, Gavin acted as if he were dusting them off. "After a week like this, I think the two of us deserve some ice cold sodas."

I chuckled. "Make mine orange and you got a deal."

At that moment, the crowd in the cafeteria exploded with applause and cheers. I'm not sure why, but my throat tightened up. It might've been because my whole week had been a nonstop roller coaster of terrible-ness.

In my mind, I went down the list of which achievements we had unlocked – the kid in the hockey mask had been caught, everyone in the talent show was saved from getting drenched in paint, the talent show itself was still on for the day, the kids behind the evil scheme had been caught, Hotcakes had been returned *safely* to his cage, my ninja clan was going to have a new place to train, and a mysterious white ninja appeared who was on *my* side!

I breathed a sigh of relief at the thought of all the good we had accomplished. And whatever was happening in the cafeteria at that moment couldn't have been bad, since all we could hear were shouts of joy, right?

The door cracked open an inch, and Faith poked her head out. "You guys gotta see this," she said, upset.

Gavin pulled open the door and stepped through while I followed behind him. The crowd of cheering kids continued as we slowly made our way around the cafeteria until the stage was in full view of where we were standing.

On the stage was the cage with Hotcakes inside of it. Standing next to the cage was Wyatt, waving to the crowd. And next to Wyatt, stood Sebastian, holding a microphone in his hand and smiling like a hero.

"This is such a glorious day!" Sebastian said into the

microphone, his voice booming from the speakers. "Buchanan's very own hall monitor captain has found the missing penguin and returned it to safety!"

The sixth graders applauded again. Strange how quickly they were able to forget all the terrible things Wyatt had done. I almost envied their forgetfulness.

Sebastian turned his body as he continued delivering his speech. "I want everyone in here to know that good deeds do *not* go unnoticed, and that bad kids *can* become good!"

"What's he gonna…" Faith whispered, trailing off.

"And that's why I'd like to announce that I'm promoting Wyatt to *Vice President of Buchanan School!*" Sebastian said joyfully.

Everyone in the room shouted with "hip hip hoorays." Students were going so crazy about Hotcakes being rescued that a few of them even fainted.

"What!" Zoe shouted, but her voice was drowned out by all the shouting. "Can he do that?"

Gavin folded his arms. "Sebastian does whatever he wants in this school. Principal Davis doesn't seem to care if it doesn't cause any trouble."

"Um, Wyatt being the Vice President of our school sounds like trouble to me!" Zoe said.

Faith shot a look of disbelief at me. "Is this really happening?"

I didn't know what to say so I shrugged my shoulders. It was still early in the morning, and I had already gone through *so much* stuff that it really *did* feel like a dream.

Sebastian tapped on the microphone, and spoke. "So let's all celebrate with an amazing talent show put on by one of Buchanan's most prized students – Zoe!"

The spotlight swung around the room and landed on her. She stood at attention and blinked in silence for a second. She glanced back at me before doing anything.

"The show must go on, right?" I said, shrugging my shoulders. "I'll be fine."

Zoe's expression shifted to curiosity.

"A real hero doesn't need to take credit for every good thing they do," I said, repeating her words.

My cousin's face flashed a smile. Her mouth didn't say thank you, but her eyes did. After grabbing a microphone from a nearby stand, she jogged to the front of the cafeteria as she welcomed everyone to the talent show.

Gavin and Faith sat on the metal chairs next to the soundboard.

I leaned against the back wall of the cafeteria, watching Wyatt step off the stage. Carlyle and a bunch of red ninjas in their street clothes met him at the steps, congratulating him for being named Vice President of Buchanan.

I saved the day yet again and nobody even noticed. If I wasn't in the right place at the right time, there would be a roomful of sobbing students covered in paint, and I wasn't even going to get as much as a nod of approval from anyone. Part of me felt sad about it, but that feeling passed quickly when I remembered Zoe's words.

Being a ninja isn't about fame and popularity; it's about honor, loyalty, and family. Once I realized that, the sad feeling I had sorta just… vanished.

Letting my eyes drift across the room, I saw Zoe on the stage cracking jokes and making kids laugh as she started the show. She was a natural performer, that was for sure. Everyone in the room was there simply because my cousin wanted to throw a crazy party in the form of a talent show. She wasn't doing this for herself; she was doing it for the students of Buchanan.

Wyatt was off to the side of the cafeteria. I know because I kept my eye on him the whole time Zoe spoke. But then I suddenly realized something else…

I *wasn't* angry.

Sure, this had been an awful week for me with an almost nonstop shower of terror soaking me to my bones, but as I watched my cousin on the stage, all those angry feelings disappeared. Zoe was smiling – *really smiling*, and that was when I became aware of the fact that I didn't care if Wyatt got credit for finding Hotcakes.

So what? It's more important that Hotcakes was safe and unhurt. If Wyatt got credit for it, then so be it. It might seem unfair, but honestly, I'm just happy that Sophia can rest easy knowing her pet, that she *loves*, is safe.

President Sebastian promoting Wyatt to Vice President was another thing. It was crazy obvious that something was going on there, and that their part of the story was *far* from over, but standing in the cafeteria at that moment, I chucked a short laugh and shook my head. Whatever was happening could wait until the next week. If I just stewed on my anger, then I'd miss out on the things that mattered and made me happy. And for me, it was seeing my cousin confidently talking on stage to a whole school of sixth graders.

I smiled again. Coincidently, Faith made eye contact and smiled at me right at that second. I'm glad the room was dark because I'm pretty sure I blushed.

I had a goofy grin on my face, but the truth was that the penguin was safe, Zoe was happy, and the talent show could go on exactly as planned. My cousin was about to put on a killer show, and I was able to watch it. Life was alright, no... life was *good*.

And to me, that was worth way more than a thousand bucks.

Stories – what an incredible way to open one's mind to a fantastic world of adventure. It's my hope that this story has inspired you in some way, lighting a fire that maybe you didn't know you had. Keep that flame burning no matter what. It represents your sense of adventure and creativity, and that's something nobody can take from you. Thanks for reading! If you enjoyed this book, I ask that you help spread the word by sharing it or leaving an honest review!

- Marcus
m@MarcusEmerson.com

THESE BOOKS HAVE SO MUCH AWESOME THAT YOU'LL
BE LIKE, "WHOA! THAT WAS **ALOT** OF AWESOME!
THAT WAS SO MUCH AWESOME THAT I ACTUALLY
HAVE A BUNCH OF LEFTOVER AWESOME! NOW WHAT
AM I GONNA DO WITH ALL THIS **EXTRA** AWESOME??"

I'LL TELL YOU WHAT YOU'RE GONNA DO! YOU'RE
GONNA GO OUT AND YOU'RE GONNA **BE** AWESOME!
THAT'S WHAT!

Marcus Emerson is the author of several highly imaginative children's books including the 6th Grade Ninja series, Secret Agent 6th Grader, Lunchroom Wars, and the Adventure Club Series. His goal is to create children's books that are engaging, funny, and inspirational for kids of all ages - even the adults who secretly never grew up.

Born and raised in Colorado Springs, Marcus Emerson is currently having the time of his life with his beautiful wife Anna and their three amazing children. He still dreams of becoming an astronaut someday and walking on Mars.